"I'm just not ready for this, Bret," Cassie said, opening the door. "I have to go."

Before he could consider the rashness of his action, Bret's hand shot out and pushed the door shut. When Cassie whirled to face him, her blue eyes flaring, he pulled her into his arms and lowered his mouth to hers, stifling her protest.

Cassie tried to be outraged, but something deep within her was glad he wouldn't let her go. She felt a primitive thrill at finding him strong enough, caring enough, to knock down the barriers of her fears.

At first the kiss was forceful, almost bruising, a statement that he was prepared to crush any resistance. But as Cassie's lips parted and softened, he gentled. "Cassie," he whispered, scarcely releasing her lips as he spoke, turning her name into a verbal caress.

Cassie's arm crept upward to twine around his neck. The onslaught of sensation was like a huge breaker catching her with such power she could only ride its crest and revel in the exhilaration of the adventure. She couldn't think. For once, she wanted only to feel. . . .

WHAT ARE *LOVESWEPT* ROMANCES?

They are stories of true romance and touching emotion. We believe those two very important ingredients are constants in our highly sensual and very believable stories in the *LOVESWEPT* line. Our goal is to give you, the reader, stories of consistently high quality that may sometimes make you laugh, sometimes make you cry, but are always fresh and creative and contain many delightful surprises within their pages.

Most romance fans read an enormous number of books. Those they truly love, they keep. Others may be traded with friends and soon forgotten. We hope that each *LOVESWEPT* romance will be a treasure—a "keeper." We will always try to publish

LOVE STORIES YOU'LL NEVER FORGET
BY AUTHORS YOU'LL ALWAYS REMEMBER

The Editors

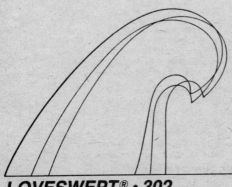

LOVESWEPT® • 302

Gail Douglas
Flirting with Danger

 BANTAM BOOKS
TORONTO • NEW YORK • LONDON • SYDNEY • AUCKLAND

FLIRTING WITH DANGER
A Bantam Book / January 1989

If you would be interested in receiving protective vinyl
covers for your Loveswept books, please write to this address
for information:

Loveswept
Bantam Books
P.O. Box 985
Hicksville, NY 11802

ISBN 0-553-21953-7

Published simultaneously in the United States and Canada

Bantam Books are published by Bantam Books, a division
of Bantam Doubleday Dell Publishing Group, Inc. Its trademark, consisting of the words "Bantam Books" and the
portrayal of a rooster, is Registered in U.S. Patent and
Trademark Office and in other countries. Marca Registrada.
Bantam Books, 666 Fifth Avenue, New York, New York 10103.

PRINTED IN THE UNITED STATES OF AMERICA

O   0 9 8 7 6 5 4 3 2 1

One

Cassie Walters tugged on the lapels of her tuxedo jacket and straightened her shoulders. She was tempted to linger in the warm glow of the September evening's sunset, where her senses were tantalized by a breeze as crisp and sweet as apple cider. But her self-discipline won out.

With determined strides she walked across the parking lot to the entrance to one of Toronto's most luxurious waterfront condominium buildings and pushed open the wide glass doors.

Spotting a pay phone in the outer lobby, Cassie headed straight for it. As she inserted a coin to make one more call to her office, she realized her hands were trembling. How silly, she scolded herself. Surely she wasn't nervous about a simple job!

Still, it took her two tries to punch out the right number, and she had to wonder: Was it the job that was bothering her, or the particular client in question? "Jan," she said when her assistant answered, "have you managed to track him down?"

"Yes and no," the young woman said. "He's home now, or someone is, because the phone's been busy since you left here. But I haven't been able to get through to him."

Cassie heaved a sigh. "Wouldn't you think a big-time businessman would be easier to reach? I'd be a lot less edgy if we could have told him that I'm replacing Max."

"Stage fright, Cass?" Jan asked.

"I feel like the curtain's about to go up, the critics are all out front, and I don't know my lines," Cassie admitted.

"It's stage fright, all right," Jan said. "Buck up, kid. You're still the best."

"I haven't so much as hefted a tray of drinks in almost a year," Cassie said. "Suddenly I'm taking our best butler's place at an important party given by our biggest client." Giving voice to her little attack of nerves didn't help. She felt worse. "Why did Max have to pick tonight to get sick? Max never gets sick! Bret Parker doesn't want any butler but Max, and he's not going to be pleased when he finds out I'm—" She clamped her lips together to stop the flow of words, annoyed that she was sounding like such a ninny. She sighed. "I guess I'll just buzz him on the intercom and try to explain I'm his butler, like it or not."

Jan laughed. "I can't believe you're in such a tizzy over this, Cass. It's not like you. What's wrong? Are you scared you'll spill a tray of drinks on the sophisticated Mr. Parker?"

"Exactly," Cassie said. "The man has influence. He could give the agency the kiss of death by deciding Jeeves is no longer the "in" service." She wasn't being totally honest. The real truth was that she'd become entirely too fascinated by Bret Parker. Though she'd never met him, she'd spoken to him on the phone many times, and he had a wonderful voice. He was also utterly charming. And every word she'd read about him—while doing her homework for business reasons, of course— had whetted her interest. Now she was about to meet him in the gorgeous flesh, and for some reason the prospect unnerved her. Bringing her thoughts back to the present, she realized Jan was saying something. "What was that?" she asked.

"I said you shouldn't try to explain things over some impersonal intercom," Jan repeated. "Just march up to Parker's apartment and give him the news face-to-face. Ten to one he'll take a look at you and forget Max Webster exists."

Cassie tried to ignore the frisson of excitement Jan's words triggered. "The man romances models and movie stars, Jan. A lady butler won't sweep him off his feet, believe me. But you're right. I'll just go up there. And I'd better go right now, so 'bye."

"Break a leg," Jan said with maddening good humor.

Cassie went through the second set of glass doors along with a tenant, who'd used his key, but she realized she couldn't go right up to Parker's apartment. The balding, paunchy man behind the concierge's desk was eyeing her suspiciously.

Pasting on a smile, Cassie approached him as his bored gaze made a quick sweep of her black tux, red bow tie, and matching cummerbund. "Hi," she said brightly. "I'm from the Jeeves Butler Agency. Mr. Parker, in twenty-three eleven, is expecting me." An inconsequential little fib, she told herself. Mr. Parker was expecting Max.

The concierge immediately challenged her slip. "Mr. Parker's expecting Max Webster," he said. "That getup you're wearing is the same as Max's, but you sure don't look like him."

Cassie sighed inwardly, and her smile turned plastic as she whipped out her Jeeves identification card and placed it on the desk. "Max isn't feeling well," she explained, trying very hard to appreciate that the concierge's duty was to protect the building's tenants. "I'm the replacement," she added.

There was a mirror behind the desk. Cassie stole a quick peek at herself while the man carefully examined her ID. Her makeup was intact, she noted, her dark hair still pulled neatly back in its French braid, no willful curls escaping.

Finally the man looked up at her. He was frowning as he pushed the card back to her. "I hope Max is okay."

It took Cassie a moment to realize his frown had been one of concern, not suspicion. "He's picked up that awful flu that's been making the rounds," she answered with a more genuine smile.

"Well," the concierge said, glancing past her to be sure another person who had just entered his lobby wasn't an intruder, "I guess you can go right on up to Mr. Parker's apartment."

Cassie pocketed her ID card and flashed one more smile at the man, just for good measure. "Thanks," she murmured, pivoting on her heel and heading for the elevators.

"Give Max my best," the concierge called after her.

She looked back at him. "I'll do that," she promised, wondering again what Max Webster's secret was. Everybody loved him. Including, she thought with a slightly sinking heart, Bret Parker. The man never planned a function until he'd made sure Max was available.

She pressed the elevator button and told herself she'd just have to show Mr. Parker that Max wasn't the only competent Jeeves butler around.

She was surprised she wasn't more tired. The day had been an endless administrative nightmare, and now she was facing an important Bret Parker party. This one wasn't a mere celebrity bash, but the engagement celebration for Parker's sister.

Max had been fussing over the arrangements for weeks. Cassie smiled. If Max had said it once, he'd said it dozens of times: "Mr. Parker wants everything to be perfect. His family means the world to him. He can't do enough for them. We don't want to let him down."

Right, Max, she told him silently, as she'd told him again and again on the phone. We won't let Mr. Parker down. And I won't let you down, Max. She hadn't realized what a fussbudget her top employee could be.

Jeeves, her little, one-woman operation, obviously the right idea in the right place at the right time, had begun expanding two years before into a full-fledged company, and Max had almost seemed like the cavalry riding to her rescue.

By now she'd acquired a whole staff of butlers, but Cassie still saw Max as the agency's mainstay. So did he, as a matter of fact, she thought with a smile.

The elevator doors slid open at the twenty-third floor, and Cassie realized she'd been so deep in thought, she'd hardly been aware of being whisked up there. She found twenty-three eleven and gave herself one last little pep talk: Butlering was like bike riding—once learned, never forgotten. If Bret Parker decided to be difficult about the substitution, she could handle it. Lifting the door's brass knocker, she gave three firm taps.

There was no response. Cassie scowled. Why the busy phone line if Parker wasn't home? she wondered. He had to be home.

She knocked again.

No one answered. Her slight nervousness turned

to slight irritation. What was she supposed to do now?

Suddenly a voice from above spoke in a familiar deep baritone. Cassie let go of the knocker and jumped back, startled.

"The door's not locked, Max," he said. "Could you let yourself in?"

Cassie put her hand on the knob, peering all around the doorway. Spooky, she thought. Her own building had an intercom from the lobby, but not from the apartment to the hallway. Was Bret Parker big on security and electronic gadgetry, just like her father? It wasn't a comforting thought. If Bret Parker was anything like Fred Walters in other ways, she might well be in for a real scene. Why did high-powered people so often have to be temperamental?

With a deep breath, she opened the door and stepped inside, trying not to be negative before even meeting the client. He was awfully casual, she reasoned, but what did she expect? To be greeted by a butler? *She* was the butler!

"I'm in the kitchen, Max," the rich male voice called.

Cassie followed the sound. Great apartment, she noted on the way through. The muted gray-and-white color scheme, the sleek furniture, and bold watercolor originals on the walls somehow managed to create a cozy if ultramodern atmosphere. Almost as if the person living there were . . . nice. But was it likely a man who had risen from construction worker to tycoon in a few short years would be 'nice'?

Well, why not? she thought with a tiny smile. She was beginning to be as amused by her agitated state as Jan.

The beautifully resonant voice spoke again, but not to Cassie. Was the man *still* on the phone?

She hesitated to go into the kitchen, afraid of walking in on a big business deal or a long-distance flirtation. What if Parker weren't dressed?

Her heartbeat suddenly became erratic, and she was shocked by her forbidden thoughts.

At the kitchen doorway, both Cassie and her heartbeat stopped.

She was too professional to ignore completely the airy, well-equipped room, but it was merely a blurred backdrop for the single dominating feature: Bret Parker himself.

The photographs she'd seen of him didn't do him justice, Cassie realized instantly. They did portray his strong features, of course—the man's bone structure seemed to have been carved by a sure hand that favored the uncompromisingly masculine lines cameras loved.

Photos only hinted at his larger-than-life size, at the barely contained energy and power that was typical of dynamic men like Bret Parker.

However, pictures couldn't capture the lightning-bolt impact of the man, the force field that drained Cassie's strength as a power magnet erases a video tape.

She leaned against the doorjamb, her legs suddenly rubbery. His attention focused elsewhere, he didn't see her at first, and she was glad.

Cassie took in the scene slowly, all her preconceptions about Bret Parker whirling aimlessly through her brain. To her dismay, deep-seated longings she'd tried to keep buried were suddenly released to assert their existence and mock her denial.

Nevertheless, Cassie couldn't help smiling. Was this man the urbane bachelor of the gossip columns, the daring entrepreneur who, at thirty-three, was startling the staid establishment with his success and defiantly bold style? The ultimate

Yuppie, with the carefully cultivated image, complete with designer suits and snappy sports car?

Clad only in faded jeans, this real-life version of Bret Parker stood in bare feet, his long, muscular legs planted astride, taut thighs straining at the soft, well-washed denim. He was dressed—barely—and he was a sight to behold.

Cassie didn't even try to breathe as her gaze lingered over broad shoulders, an iron wall of chest, a narrow waist, and lean hips. Bronze skin, satiny smooth, made her hands tingle.

She was twenty-seven years old, and not a complete stranger to attraction or desire—though she'd kept such feelings at bay without much difficulty. But never in her life had she experienced the almost-irresistible impulse simply to slide her palms over a male torso as she wanted to touch this Titan of a man whose arms looked as if they could crush stone pillars . . . or a woman's body.

What really got to her was the rest of the picture: He stood in the middle of the kitchen beside a table that was draped in quilted, bunny-printed plastic, calmly, competently changing a baby's diaper. He was also talking in a low voice to his tiny charge, and the two of them were smiling at each other in mutual affection.

Unbidden tears pricked at Cassie's eyelids as her attention focused on the child, an adorable little boy that she judged to be a little over a year old, his chubby arms and legs waving like a confused windmill, his eyes dark and full of mischief. A giggle rolled up from his fat tummy through his body to escape his mouth in a kind of hiccup.

It occurred to Cassie that the sculptors of ancient statuary had missed a bet. There was something especially magnificent about such invincible, godlike male strength harnessed for tenderness.

A discus thrower was interesting; a powerful man smiling down at an infant was moving.

And Cassie, though she tried not to succumb to such sentimentalism, was deeply moved.

With a sprinkle of sweet-smelling baby powder, the job was done just as Cassie gasped for air.

At the sound, Bret turned his head, pinioning her with a gaze that was at first puzzled, then unreadable.

Cassie's hand went to her throat, one finger tugging at her suddenly tight collar. Her mouth was dry; she tried to swallow, then ran the tip of her tongue over her lips, all the while transfixed by burnt-sienna eyes that searched and probed with startling intensity. Cassie was shaken. She wondered what he was seeing, how much he was seeing, how deeply into her secret, hidden layers.

Bret wasn't sure what he was seeing. Or thinking. Or feeling. But suddenly his world seemed to have tilted by several degrees and he found himself concentrating on luminous midnight-blue eyes as if they were his new center of gravity.

A strange sense of recognition nagged at him. He couldn't understand it. He wasn't a mystical man, not superstitious, or given to belief in destiny, fate, people being meant for each other. Love at first sight, for instance, was a lot of foolishness.

He swallowed hard. Why, then, did he feel as if this moment had been preordained? Why were his insides churning with excitement and inexplicable anticipation?

He actually found himself struck by a crazy thought, the dumbest and corniest line in existence: Where had she been all his life?

He studied the slender form in the kitchen doorway, every fiber of his body responding to her translucent ivory skin, delicate features in an oval face, inviting lips.

Trying not to take his sudden insanity too seriously, he toyed with the idea that the woman was just a figment of his imagination. She wasn't really there at all.

If so, he'd conjured up a puzzling vision. He liked females with soft, pale, slightly untamed curls; this creature's hair was blue-black and sleek. He favored gentle goddesses, pliant and fluid, drifting through his dreams in gowns the color of the sea. So why was he knocked out by this man-tailored, crisp-looking . . .?

All at once he recognized the signature Jeeves tuxedo. "You're not Max," he protested aloud, totally disoriented, utterly confused.

Cassie's gaze slid upward from the burnished-gold body to his eyes, which were flickering with copper flames, then farther up, to his neatly clipped but rumpled auburn hair, then back down to the V-shaped thatch of chest hair in the same reddish-brown shade, and finally again to his mesmerizing eyes. "'No," she said at last, her voice barely above a whisper. She forgot the explanations she'd prepared, the soothing phrases designed to ward off the client's anger. "I'm not Max. I'm Cassie."

Bret's thinking processes seemed to have gone on hold. Then something rang a bell, something vague. "Cassie," he repeated softly. "Short for Cassandra?"

She nodded.

"Pretty name," Bret murmured, still in a fog.

"Thank you," Cassie said with difficulty, her body turning to liquid warmth at the small compliment. He liked her name. Her spirits took flight.

A small, irritating voice of sanity that rarely left her alone began clamoring for attention. How many other women, it insistently reminded her, had this man devastated that day? And wasn't her awed response to Bret Parker exactly what she'd been afraid of? Cassie fought for self-control. "My mother does a lot of reading," she explained, keeping her tone light. "Mother was in her classical mode when I was born." Hearing her own self-deprecating comment helped dissipate the trance. "It could have been worse," she added with a stab at humor. "I might have been saddled with Medusa, or something."

"Never," Bret returned without hesitation. "Your mother knew what she was doing. I remember enough of my Homer to know that Cassandra was the most beautiful of the daughters of King Priam of Troy."

Practiced charm, Cassie tried to tell herself. The man was known for it. But oh, he was smooth, she thought.

She *had* to pull herself together. "Mr. Parker," she said, forcing herself to get down to business, "I tried to reach you all afternoon. Then my assistant started calling, but your line has been busy."

The baby, obviously deciding he'd been ignored long enough, chose that moment to deliver a kick to Bret's stomach, forcing Cassie to suppress a smile and drawing her glance to the flat expanse of muscle and sinew. She watched in helpless fascination as a large hand closed over the tiny foot and brought it upward to sculptured lips for a noisy kiss.

Her throat closed over as he scooped up the baby, cradling him in one prizefighter-sized arm; her pulse raced as Bret Parker moved with pantherlike grace to the wall phone and picked up the receiver, tilting his head to one side to listen. How could such an ordinary action, Cassie asked herself, make her senses reel? Why was a man's ease with a baby striking such responsive chords in the hidden recesses of her being? She'd long since decided that the nest-building syndrome wasn't for her.

Bret frowned and hung up. "I guess the receiver must be off the hook in the bedroom. We must have knocked against the phone when we were in there roughhousing a while ago. And I was out of touch all afternoon because I took Slugger for an outing. Why were you trying to reach me?"

Roughhousing with a baby, Cassie thought. How . . . nice. She barely heard his question, all her awareness concentrated on the soft, plump bundle of helplessness snuggling contentedly against the most blatant, raw masculinity she'd ever seen. "What?" she asked vaguely, his words not fully penetrating. She kept thinking about Parker's reputation as a womanizing power broker. Yet he'd taken the afternoon off from making deals and seducing women to take a baby for an outing. The two images didn't fit together.

Bret felt as if Cassie's velvety gaze were physically stroking his skin. The warm visual caress had its inevitable effect, and he had to turn his back on her, lifting the baby to his shoulder to be jiggled and patted as if for a burping, though the child had been fed much too long before to need to be burped. "Why were you calling me?" he asked again.

Huge dark eyes peered over Bret's shoulder at Cassie, and the cherubic mouth curved in a friendly smile. Then the energetic movements and back-patting inspired a tuneless song, vibrating on one note with lusty enthusiasm.

"I . . . I'm afraid Max is sick," Cassie said carefully, remembering to brace herself for an explosion.

Bret turned and stared at her. "You mean you're . . ." He paused, realizing he'd forgotten why he'd kept his back to Cassie in the first place. But his body had settled down a bit, his physical responses back under control. The baby hadn't settled down at all. He was a budding Pavarotti.

"Perhaps if you stopped . . . um . . . jiggling him," Cassie suggested, trying not to laugh. She had to shout to be heard, and it amazed her once again how tiny bodies could generate such volume.

Belatedly aware of the compulsive bouncing that had inspired the baby's joyous outburst, Bret stopped; so did the singing.

"Max is sick," Cassie said, then blurted out the rest, getting it over with. "I'm taking his place."

"You mean you're my butler?" Bret asked, feeling rotten about his delight. Poor Max was sick, he had to remember.

For a reason Cassie didn't care to explore, his use of *my* and an odd pleasure in his tone sent a subtle but supercharged thrill buzzing along her spine. She struggled to ignore it. "I assure you," she said in her best professional voice, "I'm well trained and quite experienced."

Bret's mouth quirked in a grin as he decided her formality was endearing. Especially considering the highly informal way she kept looking at him.

Her identity finally hit him. "You're Cassie Walters," he said. "Not a part-time substitute. I've talked to you on the phone a few times. You own Jeeves. You're the founder, Max's boss." His grin broadened. "I'm honored. The company president is my butler."

Right on cue the baby squirmed around to take another look at Cassie, studying her as if to decide whether she was up to the job.

For some silly reason Cassie hoped she was getting the little imp's seal of approval, and her spine tingled again at Bret's slightly possessive use of *my butler.*

She was lost for words. She hadn't expected Bret Parker to be reasonable, much less pleased. But to say he was "honored"! "You're being very understanding," she said guardedly. This was too good to be true, she thought to herself.

Bret remembered his manners. "What's wrong with Max?"

"He has the flu," Cassie replied. "In fact, my regular staff has been decimated by the epidemic, and I didn't want to send you a part-time butler. I mean," she added hastily, "our occasional people are wonderful—very competent—but . . ."

Bret waited, smiling.

Heavens, even his teeth were beautiful, Cassie thought helplessly as she went on with her explanation. "Anyway," she said lamely, "Max was so upset about letting you down, I promised I'd handle the assignment personally."

"That's good of you," Bret said. He couldn't stop grinning. "Both of you. But I hope Max isn't lying in bed fussing about it. I don't mean to down-play the importance of what he does—or what you do—but in the grand scheme of things a person's health matters more than any party."

The man was everything Max had claimed and more, Cassie decided. He was also everything she'd feared . . . and more.

She reined in her runaway emotions. It simply wouldn't do for the president of Jeeves to fall for the agency's best-known client.

Get to the job at hand, her inner voice reminded her. A Jeeves butler was supposed to be a regular Bernstein of entertaining, conducting a virtual symphony of a party. There was precious little time for mooning over the client. She simply had to start working.

The baby chose that moment to twist his body around on the broad shoulder and fling himself toward Cassie, arms outstretched.

Instinctively, her hands flew up to catch him, her reaction lightning-quick.

But Bret had a firm grip on the small body, and the baby laughed delightedly, throwing himself back against the solid chest, then repeating the whole process twice more in a teasing game of peekaboo.

Little ham, Cassie thought silently. But she couldn't help grinning back at him. The child's dark, laughing eyes were filled with taunting glee.

Bret was intrigued by her instant readiness to catch the child. She'd obviously been around youngsters a lot. Was she a mother? She wasn't wearing a wedding band. Interesting. "What's this, Slugger?" he asked. "Are you flirting with our butler?"

The reply was an excited giggle and an unintelligible speech directed at Cassie.

"Easy for you to say, Slugger," she said playfully. The little boy nestled against Bret again, apparently talked out.

"Is he yours?" Cassie asked, mainly to fill the awkward silence. "Or," she added with a half-smile, "did he come with the condo? You never know nowadays, what with all these package deals." She'd never read that Bret Parker had children. Was Slugger a big secret?

Bret laughed easily, glad his dream lady had a sense of humor. "Slugger's my nephew. His parents are in town for the party. They live in Buffalo. Since they wanted to see some friends and their baby-sitter wasn't available for the afternoon, Uncle Bret was commandeered."

Uncle Bret, Cassie repeated silently. It didn't fit the media's image of him at all. He was becoming more dangerously devastating by the second, and she'd promised herself she wouldn't be devastated by him. She cleared her throat and searched for something harmless to say. "Is his name really Slugger?"

"John, actually. Johnny, to his mother. He was named for his dad, my brother Jack. I call him Slugger in the hope he'll grow up with a great batting stance and help out the Blue Jays." With his free hand, Bret began clearing the table of the diaper-changing paraphernalia, aware that the work space would be needed by the caterers.

Cassie pitched in to help, putting the baby powder into a blue diaper bag and fitting the cap onto a lotion jar. "You think names affect destinies?" she asked idly.

"Have you ever heard of Attila the Accountant?" Bret shot back with a grin. "Conan the Couturier?"

"You have a point," Cassie said. He wasn't helping her get rid of her silly smile. And did he have to be amusing along with everything else? she asked the heavens. The man didn't play fair. No wonder women flocked to him like kids to the Pied Piper. Cassie Walters was practically immune to notorious male charmers, yet she was bowled over!

"Anyway," he added, "the name-and-destiny theory is proven by your own case. Cassandra is the name of a beautiful woman, remember?"

Cassie wanted to laugh off that remark, but he sounded almost shy, utterly disarming her, making her cheeks flood with color. The situation was getting serious. Reaching into her breast pocket for a small notebook, she flipped it open and hoped a brisk, businesslike attitude would make up for her adolescent blushing. "The caterers will be here soon," she said, pressing her lips together as the lower one threatened to tremble. "I really must start getting ready for them. Max gave me a run-down on where to find things here, Mr. Parker, so . . ."

He took the hint. "I'll get out of your way, then," he said as he stroked the back of the baby's head. Anyway, he decided, it was time to get Slugger into his Dr. Dentons and ready for his rendezvous with the evening's sitter.

Cassie looked up briefly and gave Bret a distant smile, hoping to give the impression she already was lost in serious thought.

But after he'd left the kitchen she kept seeing him standing there holding his lovable nephew, unconsciously affectionate with the child, strong enough to be gentle, his expressive amber eyes still mesmerizing her, disturbing her. Both males had shaken up her tidy world as it hadn't been shaken in a long time.

Two

To the interested amusement of certain members of the Parker clan, the host and butler for the Karen Parker–Russ Hamilton engagement party were noticeably distracted.

Bret, finding his glance constantly straying to the lithe form in the Jeeves tux, was confused by his absorption with Cassie Walters. She was lovely enough to inspire the interest of any man, but no more so than most of the other women who had wandered through his life during the past couple of years with little impact. Yet somehow he knew she mattered to him in a strange, special way.

For her part, Cassie had gotten right into the swing of her job, so she couldn't blame stage fright for her feelings.

In fact, she was *too* comfortable with her work. It didn't occupy enough of her attention. At every moment she was acutely aware of the party's host and beginning to feel as if she'd grabbed a live wire and couldn't let go. Thinking back to the way she'd reacted to the first realization that she'd have to stand in for Max at this party, she half-believed in portents and omens, though it wasn't like her to indulge in such fancies. But she'd actually sensed somehow that meeting Bret Parker could upset the tidy little apple cart of her carefully staged existence. She'd made a lot of plans for herself, and they didn't allow for close encounters of any kind. So it was a real problem that each time her wayward gaze flickered around the room to alight on Bret Parker and, incredibly, met the wondrous intensity of his hypnotic eyes, another jolt of electricity sang through her.

It should have helped that the man who had emerged from his bedroom in urbane black tie was the image she'd had all along of Bret Parker. He was not her type. Of course not, she told herself. Why, he was clearly the hunk the media showed him to be, and Cassie was definitely leery of hunks. Especially sophisticated, smooth, charming hunks. They could cause mayhem in a woman's life.

Frightening things were going on inside her. The cool, controlled woman she pretended to be was all at once beset by unaccountable trembling, by heat flashing through her, by butterflies in her stomach.

She started hoping she was coming down with the flu.

But none of the flu symptoms she'd heard about included sweet music, yet every time she found herself captured by his gaze her heartstrings glided through an arpeggio that didn't come from the strolling guitarist hired for the evening. Cassie could almost see some mischievous Cupid serenading her with his little harp.

And the Cupid looked exactly like Slugger.

A shiver of glasses on the large silver tray she was carrying reminded her that she had to keep her mind on the job. It was the third time she'd come perilously close to tipping the tray. Such unprofessional behavior wasn't at all like her. It had to be the flu, music or no music, she decided.

Bret, she noticed, was chatting with his two sisters, across the room. Cassie made up her mind that she had to treat him as just another client. She would work her way toward him with her tray of drinks instead of dispatching a waiter. It was important to prove to herself that her temporary insanity had no effect on her work.

"There's been a theft," Karen Parker announced to her sister, grinning.

"Hmm," Bret murmured absently, his gaze and mind on Cassie Walters as she moved smoothly through the crowd, at once unobtrusive and charming, not as showy as Max, but a perfect butler in her own way, all efficiency and dignity and attentiveness.

Suddenly he noticed a hand waving in front of his eyes.

He blinked. The hand was Karen's. He realized she'd said something. Something about a theft. "What was that?" he demanded, startled. "What theft? When? What are you talking about?"

Karen shook her head and sighed deeply, turning to Patricia, the oldest of the Parker brood. "Didn't I tell you, Trish?" Karen said, her brown eyes sparkling. "The man's completely out of it."

"What theft?" Bret repeated, alarmed.

Trish put her hand on his arm. A tall, cool, elegant blonde, Patricia was the unofficial family peacemaker. "Karen's baiting you," she explained with a quirk of her lips. "Little sister is taking her revenge for all your teasing when she fell for Russ."

Bret scowled. "You've lost me. I don't get the connection."

"As I said," Karen put in. "He's out of it."

"What theft?" Bret asked insistently.

"Your heart," Trish answered.

"Your senses," Karen amended. "You've turned into a love-sick zombie before our eyes. I always knew you'd fall eventually, but at my engagement party?" A petite blonde version of her older sister but with more fire than ice about her, Karen was the unofficial family troublemaker. She especially loved teasing her beloved older brother. "This is supposed to be *my* night, remember?"

Bret looked from one sister to the other and couldn't think of a word to say. Was he so transparent? "Look," he muttered, "just because I happen to admire a pretty woman . . ."

"He's blushing," Karen said. "See, Trish? He's actually scarlet! Isn't that sweet?"

"Who's scarlet?" their sister-in-law asked, joining them.

Bret knew he was outnumbered and considered beating a hasty retreat, but didn't want to give Karen the satisfaction, so he smiled at Jack's wife, Susan. A Dresden-doll type with thick ash-brown hair, huge green eyes, and a deceptively innocent sweetness about her, Susan was in her own way as much a minx as Karen.

"Who's scarlet?" Susan persisted, then trained her wide-eyed look on Bret. "Why, for heaven's sake, I hope you're not coming down with something, you poor dear. Did the baby wear out his uncle after all?"

"I'm fine," Bret said, still smiling but through clenched teeth. "Just suffering the usual overdose of Nosy Parkers."

"I'll tell you who's sent him into shock," Karen said in a stage whisper. "It's like any decent parlor mystery. The butler did it."

Bret glared at her. "You're not too big to spank, Karen."

She laughed, not terribly concerned. "Just don't go treating this lady the way you've been treating the others, if she's reckless enough to get involved with you. Ms. Jeeves seems to be the vulnerable type, and you, Mr. Tough Guy, have recently turned into a positive menace to womankind. I love you dearly, but—"

Bret's look turned thunderous. "What's that remark supposed to mean?"

"Women, Porsches, Italian suits—all part of the image, nothing more. Good old Elizabeth did her number on you and turned you into a regular Don Juan." Karen took a sidelong peek at Cassie, across the room. "Maybe you'll be snapping out of this phase soon, though," she added with a knowing grin.

Karen's comments bothered Bret more than he wanted to admit. As a rule he was cautious to confine himself to women as uncaring as himself. With them it was easy to say good night at the door, exchange no empty promises, endure no hassles, feel no guilt. But he had to admit he'd hurt a few women's feelings by misjudging situations, and he wasn't proud of it.

Karen was right, he thought. Cassie was one of the vulnerable ones. The kind he steered clear of.

She was also approaching, he suddenly realized. "Ms. Jeeves is heading our way," he muttered. "So button your lip, little sister, or I'll tell your bridegroom what you're like in the morning."

Karen made a childish face. "You always did play dirty, Bret Parker." Nevertheless she turned to the others and changed the subject.

Bret couldn't help smiling as Cassie drew near. Her very presence gave him strange little bursts of happiness. But it troubled him that Karen had spotted his feelings so easily. In fact, it troubled him that he had such feelings.

When Cassie held out her tray, Bret replaced his empty glass with a fresh drink and glanced around the room in search of a good excuse for a getaway. To his pleased surprise a perfect one presented itself almost immediately. "Uh-oh," he said, touching Karen's shoulder. "I see Russ has been buttonholed by Uncle George. I'd better rescue the poor kid. George is a good man but—"

"Bor-ing," the three women said in unison, then laughed.

Cassie kept her expression impassive as another onslaught of unfamiliar emotions hit her. She felt bereft, cheated of Bret's presence as if deprived of a basic necessity of life, yet she was relieved. His nearness seriously undermined her butlerish detachment, not to mention making her knees wobbly.

She noticed Karen Parker's gaze was intent on her and was instantly, foolishly afraid the young woman could read her thoughts—her wicked thoughts. For Cassie's imagination, always quite well developed, thanks to a rather solitary childhood, had taken an erotic turn that night that shocked her. Her mind was like a screen with X-rated films flickering over it, and she couldn't seem to activate her censor. Was it possible that her eyes were mirroring the wild mental images she couldn't banish?

She gave Karen a quick smile and went on to other guests as fast as decent manners allowed, hoping against hope that Bret's sister couldn't see past her facade. The very thought of anyone knowing that Bret starred in her erotic fantasies was mortifying! It occurred to her she'd always been a fake: Cassie the perfect lady on the surface, another Cassie entirely on the inside.

Suddenly she felt a deep pang of sadness. It still hurt, much as she hated to admit it, that when her parents finally had been faced with the real Cassie, the one with beliefs, ambitions, and a life of her own, they hadn't been able to accept her—especially not her father. Of course, she had a few problems accepting things about him, too, she had to admit.

Banishing those pointless rehashings of old issues, she concentrated on living up to Max Webster's image.

By the time all the guests except a few members of the immediate family had left and the cleanup had been taken care of, it was midnight. There was no further need for Cassie to stay.

Bret knew the family chatter could go on half the night, and though he longed to have a few moments alone with Cassie, he knew it wasn't fair to keep her when she'd finished her job.

In a way, he told himself, it would be a relief when she'd gone. She was driving him crazy with her midnight-ocean eyes and lips that tempted him beyond reason.

He found her in the kitchen. The caterers and cleaning staff had left, their work done. "Cassie," he said, then had to pause to clear his throat before going on. Even being alone with her for a moment was almost more than he could bear. There was a physical ache in his arms and chest where her body should have been molded to his. And the kitchen held a special intimacy: It was where he'd first seen her. They could even claim their own special song: Slugger's one-note concerto.

Don't be a jerk, he told himself with a rush of annoyance. Don't get involved, he ordered. Not with this lady. "Cassie," he repeated in a cooler tone, "there's no reason for you to stick around."

She was unaccountably hurt . . . and not sure why. Had she expected him to make a pass at her? Hoped he would?

That thought shocked her more than any other, even more than the erotic adventures her mind had conjured up throughout the evening. She managed a tense smile. "I trust everything was satisfactory, Mr. Parker?"

He had to grin; she was adorable, with her prim ways. "Everything, as I'm certain you know, was perfect," he answered. "I'm sorry Max is sick, but you can assure him his boss represented him nobly." He laughed inwardly, deciding he and Cassie sounded like characters in an English drawing-room comedy. "Quite nobly," he added, playing his role to the hilt.

"Thank you," Cassie said in a small voice, glad he was pleased. Pleasing a client always mattered, but pleasing this particular client was terribly important to her.

All at once Bret knew he couldn't let her go without touching her. For want of a better idea, he thrust out his hand as he would to any business associate. "Thank *you*," he said gravely.

Cassie accepted the handshake and immediately knew it was a mistake. Warmth coursed from Bret's body into hers, traveling up her arm and spreading throughout every cell of her being. She wanted to pull away but couldn't. His fingers were strong and compelling.

"Cassie," he said again, hearing the hoarseness return to his voice. Blood was pounding in his head from the surge of raw desire that ripped through him. It took all his willpower to keep from drawing her into his arms and giving in to the lure of her soft, slightly parted lips. "Something . . ." He stopped. It was dumb even to think of saying that something important and undeniable was happening between them.

He made himself release her hand, searching his mind for an ordinary finish for his melodramatic beginning. "Something . . . uh . . . something I meant to ask you . . . it's kind of a last-minute thing . . ." How last minute he hoped she wouldn't guess: He was making it up as he went along. "Another party. On . . . on Wednesday." Max would probably still be laid up with the flu, he thought. "This Wednesday, I mean. I know you usually need advance notice, but it just came up . . . today. It'd be a simple thing. I could order trays of cold cuts and so on from a deli, if it's too late for a caterer. But I really would appreciate having a butler. If . . . if Max can't make it, could I possibly count on you? A luncheon. That's what I'm talking about. I'm trying to put together a consortium of investors for a big project I've been working on. . . ." That much was true, he mused as he extemporized his way through his impulsive plan. "Somebody suggested that a casual lunch away from the office, not in a restaurant either, would make for a better atmosphere for discussion." Not a bad idea, actually, he decided, wondering why he hadn't thought of it before. "But it's vital for everything to go smoothly, so I need you . . . or Max, of course. . . ."

Cassie's heart was pounding so violently, she was sure Bret could hear it, perhaps even see its erratic leaping right through her jacket and front-pleated white shirt.

She wondered: Would Max be on his feet by Wednesday? Did she hope so? Hope not? She hoped not, she knew in the deepest part of her. She was a horrible person, wishing such a thing on Max. And she was an idiot besides, just asking for trouble. "Of course you can count on me," she answered, praying she didn't sound as shaky as she felt. "And I'm sure our regular caterer will be able to put something together for you. If you'll call the office first thing Monday with some details about numbers and the kind of lunch you'd like served, we'll manage."

"Thanks," Bret said with deep sincerity. All he had to do now was invite the guests. Since he'd really had a meeting planned, he didn't expect trouble persuading his colleagues to get together at his place for lunch.

Then, he realized, he had to hope Max would have the sense to take his time recuperating—until after Wednesday, at least. "I really appreciate this, Cassie."

She smiled and reached into her pocket for her keys. "No problem," she murmured, excitement racing through her. She was going to see Bret again . . . as long as Max was wise enough to take a few days to recover completely from his flu. He really should. Rushing back to work would be foolish. Perhaps she'd call the poor fellow and tell him that.

"You're driving," Bret remarked, noticing Cassie's keys. "Where's your car parked?"

"In the visitor's lot."

"I'll walk you to it," Bret decided aloud.

Cassie panicked. She'd be alone with the man under a crescent moon and winking stars, the solitude of late night, the tang of early autumn in the air. . . . She wasn't quite that much of an idiot. Not yet, anyway. "Oh, no, please," she blurted out. "It's not that late, and the parking area is well lighted, and I . . . I'll be okay."

"I don't like the idea of your going down there alone at this time of night."

"It's fine, honestly," Cassie insisted. "I've managed on my own for a long time, so please don't be concerned."

Managed on her own, Bret thought. Did that mean she lived alone? He hoped so. He couldn't remember when he'd ever hoped for anything as much.

On the other hand, he *was* concerned. Naturally protective of women—having sisters had established that trait in him—he found himself overwhelmed by a fierce desire to take care of Cassie, to stop her from walking alone through parking lots late at night.

On the verge of insisting, he saw the stubborn set of her delicate jaw and realized he'd better back off. It occurred to him that Cassie hadn't carved out a successful career in a male-dominated field by being a dependent female. She obviously was less fragile than she looked. "All right," he said reluctantly, wishing he could at least tell her to call him when she was safely home, but even that was too presumptuous a request. Their relationship was strictly professional.

If his desire to protect her was sincere, he thought unhappily, their relationship would remain strictly professional. Cassie Walters didn't need a Don Juan in her life.

"Good night, Mr. Parker," she said. "Thanks for being so understanding about the last-minute change."

"On the contrary," he insisted. "Thank *you* again for covering the party yourself. I hope I'll see you Wednesday . . . I mean, if Max hasn't recovered. Not that I want him still to be . . ." Bret stopped talking before he made a total fool of himself. His acquired polish had deserted him; he was a stumbling, stuttering, nervous adolescent again. A Hollywood sex bomb he'd met the previous month hadn't reduced him to such a level. His butler had.

Cassie Walters, he told himself as he stood back and watched her leave, meant Trouble.

Bret Parker, Cassie thought as she made her escape, was pure Danger.

On Monday morning she made sure she was too busy to take his call. Hearing his voice would melt her into a little puddle, and she had work to do. She let Jan make the arrangements for his luncheon.

Max's flu was stubborn. By Wednesday Cassie knew she was going to court Danger again. She was nervous, yet couldn't suppress her excitement.

On the way to Bret's place she told herself she could handle her silly little infatuation. And surely the man's impact wouldn't be as dramatic the second time. She'd see the hard-nosed, stuffy businessman in action at this lunch, not the affectionate Uncle Bret or the indulgent brother obviously doted on by his sisters.

She was wrong. In a dark suit that didn't look remotely stuffy, Bret Parker sent her into another tailspin of excitement and barely suppressed desire. She couldn't believe what was happening to her. She'd been in firm control of her feelings for so long, she'd begun to believe herself invincible. There was no Achilles heel in her psyche.

Not until Bret Parker. The businessman was as appealing as the uncle, the brother. He wasn't a bully or a blowhard. He was enthusiastic. He was not manipulative, just persuasive.

Heaven help her, now she was not only lusting after him, she admired him! How could he be such a paragon? How could she hope to resist such a man? She didn't want to feel this way about anyone, least of all a known . . . rake.

The quaint word made her laugh at herself. Once again she was being ridiculous. Bret Parker seemed to have that effect on her.

"Thanks again," he said to her when his guests had left.

Cassie avoided the gaze that could penetrate to her long-guarded heart. "You're an important Jeeves client, Mr. Parker," she told him, mischievously imagining how he would react if she leaped on him all of a sudden and started acting out the fantasies that had been plaguing her days and nights since the previous Saturday. "Naturally I'll do everything I can for you. . . ." That didn't sound quite correct. She tried again. "I mean, to take care of your needs . . ." That was worse. "I mean . . ." She gave up. Making sense around the man was too much to expect of any mortal female.

Bret wanted so much to hold her, he didn't know how he could stop himself. But he managed, afraid of offending her if he gave in to the impulse. Cassie was reserved, proper. She wasn't cold . . . he'd glimpsed the fires under her cool surface. But she wasn't a woman who would welcome casual advances. For one thing, she was too shy.

Her shyness made him smile. It occurred to him that he'd smiled a lot during the past few days, thinking about Cassie Walters.

He wanted to see her again. Yet he shouldn't. The vibrations between them were too strong. He couldn't imagine whiling away an evening with her without their tumbling into bed, and he couldn't envision making love to her without tumbling into a deeper relationship. And wasn't he the character who had no time or inclination for deeper relationships? What if he ended up treating Cassie as if she were—what had Karen suggested? An accessory? It was an awful thought.

It was better to keep things on a butler-client basis, he told himself. Cassie Walters was an untouchable. The kind a man didn't play games with unless he had serious intentions . . . or had no conscience whatsoever. "The meeting went well," he said with studied casualness. "It was a real bonus to be able to have you here." *In more ways than one,* he added silently.

The undercurrent of tension between them was too much for Cassie. With a tiny smile, she murmured some pleasantry, turned, and bolted from the apartment. Once away from him, she vowed she would never, ever go within ten city blocks of Bret Parker for any reason. The kind of excitement she felt, she didn't need.

She spent the rest of the week in a whirlwind of activity. The staff had continued to be laid low by the flu, and she'd had to fill in at several parties after long days in the office.

"It's a wonder you don't get sick yourself," Jan said the following Tuesday as Cassie changed into her tux for another evening function.

"I keep telling myself I'm running too fast for the bug to catch me," Cassie said, bending at the waist to do the upside-down braid that kept her wild hair tamed for her assignments.

Jan went to stand behind Cassie as she straightened up, peering over her shoulder into the full-length mirror. "How do you think I'd look as a redhead?" she asked, patting her short brown hair.

"Any color seems to suit you fine," Cassie said diplomatically but honestly. She admired Jan's bold experimentation with different looks. "Red should be great on you. Auburn, maybe." Auburn, she thought, a vision of Bret Parker popping into her head. She couldn't seem to stop that from happening.

She was glad she'd been so busy lately. It helped keep her mind off him—it helped a little, but not enough. *He*, however, had obviously managed not to waste too much time sighing over *her*, judging by the gossip columns in the weekend papers. He'd been spotted at some theater opening with a glamorous woman on his arm. And Cassie had been watching a Blue Jays night game on television when the camera had panned to him and his lady friend. It was like a betrayal: Couldn't she even count on a ten-inning game against the Yankees to get her mind off the miserable man?

No, it wasn't true. He wasn't a miserable man. He was a charming man. He couldn't help it if some people took his pleasantries personally, if some people were naïve enough to think he was attracted to them.

By the following Friday Bret couldn't fight his feelings any longer. He'd tried hard enough, going out with so many women since he'd met Cassie, they'd all become a blur in his mind. And the effort hadn't done a bit of good. His thoughts kept right on straying to indigo eyes veiled by a thick fringe of dark lashes and filled with mysterious promise.

He called Max at home. The poor guy was having trouble shaking the flu. What Max probably needed, Bret reasoned, was rest. "How are you feeling?" he asked casually, swiveling in his leather chair.

"Not bad, not great," Max answered. "Why? You need me?"

"No," Bret said. "I have a proposition for you. A buddy of mine has a place in the Finger Lakes area in upstate New York. It's rustic but comfortable. He's in Europe on an extended visit, and he's been asking me to spend some time at his little retreat. He doesn't like it to be vacant for too long. I'm too busy to go down there right now, but it struck me you might find it a great spot for a bit of R and R. Interested?"

Max was interested.

Bret felt a bit guilty. Cassie was probably working too hard already, and here he was, plotting to add to her burdens—because he was going to ask her to cover for Max one more time.

Three

Cassie and Jan had their own off-the-record labels for the parties the agency organized. There were three main types: "galas," complete with bejeweled celebrities in full evening attire; "glitterings," with slightly less formal wear, not quite so many jewels, and only a sprinkling of famous people; and "festives," where ordinary, nonfamous people celebrated some special occasion.

Cassie wasn't quite sure how to label the party at Bret Parker's apartment on the second Saturday in October. The guest list definitely glittered, but the mood was informally festive, and Cassie's spirits made the whole world seem like a gala celebration.

She'd tried hard not to be thrilled to pieces when Bret had asked her—pleaded with her—to be "his" butler one more time. But she'd been so buoyant since he'd called, she'd almost felt as if she and her little van might just lift right up into the air and fly over the traffic on the way to his apartment.

She'd been puzzled as well as delighted by Bret's last-minute request for the party. It wasn't at all like him; he'd always been scrupulous about giving the agency lots of advance notice. She didn't dare suspect . . . no, that was her naïveté again, making her wish he were finding excuses to use her as his butler. It was utter folly to think that way, she told herself.

Cassie knew she could have sent a substitute for the job. Most of her full-time butlers were back at work. On the other hand, Bret had sounded *so* upset at hearing Max wasn't available, and when he'd begged her to take on just one more party for him, what could she do? The man was her agency's best client, after all. He deserved special attention.

She'd started counting the days and hours as soon as she'd hung up from his call.

The party was very private, so much so that even the catering people and waiters she'd hired hadn't known they would be serving some of the movie world's biggest stars. Several films were being made in Toronto, which had been dubbed "Hollywood North" for its rising popularity as a shooting location, and one of the producers was Bret's friend. Word had gone around the sets that a get-together without media hype was planned, so a number of the actors and crew members had dropped in to spend time with friends they laughingly admitted they rarely managed to see back in Los Angeles.

Cassie found herself slightly dazzled, though she'd served the rich and famous and even royalty more than once.

However, she'd never seen them letting their hair down, being "just folks." It was fun, she decided, to overhear delicious bits of gossip and amusing anecdotes. Household words became human beings before her eyes. She couldn't help thinking how excited her thirteen-year-old niece would be when she heard about this experience. Betsy was so star-struck.

Cassie had to battle one of her pangs of home-sickness again; she talked long-distance to her family regularly—except for her father—but she hadn't seen any of them in more than a year. A person couldn't hug over the phone, or see how much a little nephew had grown, or admire a niece's new hairstyle.

She was getting maudlin, she warned herself. Anyway, there was a positive angle to their . . . estrangement. Families could be so demanding, so time-consuming. There was always some crisis or celebration, and who needed that? Not Cassie Walters. No way.

Bret had warned her the night promised to be a late one. He'd actually suggested she ought to have an afternoon nap before coming to work. It was rather personal of him, she thought, but rather sweet, too.

As midnight passed, then one o'clock, then two, she was glad she'd taken his advice.

It was after three by the time the door was closed behind the last guest. Cassie had dismissed the staff much earlier—with difficulty, for once, since the wide-eyed waiters had been most willing to work overtime.

She cleaned up the few remaining glasses, re-turning the kitchen to its spotless, perfect order, then went to the living room to give it one last check and to remind Mr. Parker she was still around . . . in case he hadn't noticed, she thought with a tiny pout.

He was beside the wet bar, lifting the stopper of a crystal decanter of cognac.

Cassie was struck, not for the first time that evening, by how lovely it was just to look at him. No matter what he wore—now a brown tweed blazer, taupe slacks, and an open-necked, pale yellow shirt—he carried it off with easy grace.

The silence of the room suddenly underscored the fact that she was alone with Bret Parker, this time not just in her dreams. All at once breathing was a chore.

"Great party," he remarked, wondering if his voice sounded as strained to Cassie as to him. He'd waited for a chance to be alone with her. The long hours of pretending she was just a butler had taken their toll on his patience. "Once again you did Jeeves proud."

Cassie, with her usual eloquence in Bret's presence, mumbled her thanks and reached into her pocket for her keys. It was, unfortunately, time for Cinderella to say good night to the prince, she decided.

Bret saw what she was doing and grew desperate. He didn't want her to leave. It wasn't fair, not when he'd gone to so much trouble to see her. And, he had to concede, to impress her with his celebrity guests. He was like some kid showing off for a pretty girl. It was as if he'd retreated to his high-school days, when fifty quick push-ups on the football field, maybe a casual backflip or two, worked like a charm. Those had been simpler times, he mused, yet had he really gone very far beyond them?

There was so much he wanted to say to Cassie. To ask her. But all of a sudden he couldn't think. "You really did a fine job," he mumbled, cursing his blanked-out mind.

"I'm glad you were pleased," Cassie replied softly.

Bret loved her voice. It was low and sweet, as soothing as an autumn breeze. "Well, good night, Mr. Parker," she said, starting toward the doorway.

Her imminent departure snapped him out of his stupor. "The party's over, Cassie," he said bluntly, still holding the stopper of the decanter as he stood looking at her.

She tilted her head to one side, frowning. "I beg your pardon?"

"I said the party's over." Bret heard the harshness in his tone and wondered what it was about Cassie that made him revert to the old Bret Parker, the loser he thought he'd left behind. "Enough of this you-butler-me-master foolishness," he said, putting down the stopper and lifting the decanter to splash cognac into two snifters. Then he had to smile at his own awkwardness. "How about Cassie and Bret having a nightcap?" he suggested more gently.

Tempting, Cassie thought, watching the deftness of his hands as he put down the decanter and replaced the stopper. So very tempting, the prospect of sharing a middle-of-the-night cognac with Bret Parker. The stuff of fantasies, she reflected.

The thought brought back her sanity. The last thing she needed was more fuel for her fantasy existence. "I really can't," she said quietly. "But thank you."

Bret heard her refusal but saw something entirely different in the dark, infinite blue of her eyes and the instinctive softening of her lush mouth. Picking up the glasses, he walked toward her, his gaze capturing hers and challenging her to deny her real feelings.

She watched his approach with the odd sensation of being encircled by an imaginary lariat, then slowly, slowly drawn toward him as he coiled the rope around his hand until he'd shortened the distance between them.

They were inches apart. She inhaled the faint, spicy scent of his after-shave. Perhaps, she mused, if she could breathe deeply enough, his fragrance would permeate her very pores and remain with her long after she'd gone home alone.

He held out one crystal snifter, the stem between his two fingers, the globe resting lightly on their tips. Cassie took the glass, hypnotized by the flickering depths of his eyes, as richly amber as the swirling cognac.

Bret raised his glass in a silent salute.

Cassie followed his lead, then took a sip, hoping the cognac's bite would snap her out of the spell he'd cast. The impact of his nearness was sending shock waves through her, making her dizzy, tightening her throat.

But the cognac was a very good one and had no bite. It was liquid gold that filled her nostrils with its heady bouquet, heated her mouth, and soothed her throat as it slid down into her body, calming and stimulating her at the same time.

Bret watched her, fine-tuned to her responses— and to the way she fought them. He well understood the battle. He was going through one just like it. But he wondered: What were her reasons? Was she disillusioned, perhaps even a little bitter, as he was? Was honest emotion her enemy too? Or was she really just caught up in the butler-client thing? It was hard to believe anyone could be so straitlaced.

Another thought struck him. He still didn't know whether she really was free. She wasn't married or engaged; that much he'd learned for certain from Max. But she was, it seemed, such a private person, no one knew about her love life, or if she even had one. "Perhaps I'm being presumptuous," he said with a strained smile. "You don't appear to be married, but is there a jealous boyfriend lurking in the background?" His effort to make the question sound like playful banter failed. The words came out with all the urgency he felt.

Cassie blinked, taken aback. "Well, really . . . I mean . . . I don't think . . . it isn't exactly . . ."

It wasn't any of his business, he knew she was trying to tell him in a polite way. But she was wrong. It was very much his business. "There's no one, right?" he asked hopefully.

She nodded, robbed of speech. He had no right to ask, and no reason. He couldn't possibly be interested in her. It was too much to hope for.

She bit her lower lip, utterly confused. It occurred to her that she could have lied to him. She could have said there was some other man. Why hadn't she? It might have warded off a casual pass. She didn't want a casual pass from Bret Parker. Did she?

He glanced at her car keys. "I suppose you're planning to drive home alone at this hour."

Cassie nodded again, still unable to speak.

"And," he went on, "I suppose your car is in the visitor's lot again."

When Cassie's reply was another mute nod, Bret made a quick, bold decision. He reached out and took her car keys, then slipped them into his pocket.

The action loosened her tongue. "Why did you do that?" she asked, more surprised than offended or alarmed.

Bret was slightly surprised himself, but the deed was done and he wasn't sorry. "I'm afraid I can't let you go driving off by yourself in the middle of the night."

A tremor passed through Cassie. Not sure whether she was indignant, nervous, or unbearably excited, she chose to be indignant. It seemed the only proper course of action. Speaking in a tightly controlled voice, she tried to give herself a haughty air. "Mr. Parker, I happen to be a professional person. How I get home from an assignment is my concern, not yours." That sounded rude, she thought. After all, she did have to remember he was an important client. And he did mean well . . . didn't he? "It's kind of you to be concerned," she went on, "but I assure you I'm quite capable of driving home safely at any hour of the day or night. So if you'll just return my keys . . ." She held out her hand expectantly.

Bret liked her air of authority even if it didn't cut any ice with him. He looked down at her slender hand, with its graceful fingers and neatly manicured but unpolished nails. She was shaking.

In for a penny, in for a pound, he decided, taking the delicate hand in his and tugging gently, drawing Cassie toward a love seat.

It was a good name for that particular piece of furniture, he mused as he settled beside Cassie on the small couch, enjoyably close. "Kick off your shoes," he suggested. "Your feet must be aching after the night you put in."

She stared at him as if he'd lost his mind; in fact she wondered if she'd misplaced her own. What had made her follow him with such lamblike docility? "I'll have this drink," she conceded. "But then I'm leaving, keys or no keys. There are taxis, you know."

"I wish you wouldn't do that," he said quietly, not releasing her hand. He liked holding it, and she wasn't very convincing in her resistance: She wasn't pulling away. "Let me explain something, Cassie," he said, gaining confidence. "You've seen the size of this apartment. You know I have spare bedrooms. I'd like you to use one of them."

Cassie's jaw dropped.

"Don't answer yet," Bret interrupted. "I'm not making a pass at you." He began moving his thumb in slow circles on the back of her hand as he spoke softly, persuasively. "It's just that you've been kind enough to handle these last-minute parties of mine yourself, and I know you don't do that sort of thing as a rule. I can't repay you by letting you go home alone in the middle of the night. Please stay. Max would, you know. He's done it several times when parties have run late."

Cassie swallowed hard, then spoke before his touch and his gentle words made her forget herself. "Thank you. Really. Thank you. But no. You must realize that for Max to stay here isn't exactly the same as for me to do it."

Bret shrugged his shoulders. "Then I'll have to go with you and come back in a cab."

"Don't be silly," Cassie shot back, though the insistent little circles feathered over the back of her hand turned her would-be chiding into something that sounded like a breathless sigh.

Unfolding himself from the couch, Bret pulled Cassie to her feet. "Come with me," he commanded.

The guest room was an oasis of blues and greens with splashes of coral blooms—an inviting tropical pool. Cassie's resistance weakened. She *was* tired. The bed, covered with a thick coverlet, beckoned to her.

"See?" Bret said with a smile. "Total privacy. Your own bathroom, even. I'll give you a T-shirt for a nightgown." He paused, then made a solemn promise, one he knew he would have to keep no matter how he felt. "I'll say it again, Cassie. This isn't a pass. You'll be safe . . . safe from parking-lot muggers outside and amorous bachelors here. If you really believe you'd be . . . compromised . . . by staying until morning, I'll accept that, but I'll see you home."

She opened her mouth to refuse.

Bret spoke before she had a chance. "That's final, Cassandra. No arguments."

She closed her mouth. He meant it, she thought,

gazing at him in wonder. He was truly concerned about her. No one had ever offered to see her home late at night. No one had ever given her safety a second thought, no matter what time she'd left an assignment. Treasuring her independence, she'd never expected or wanted such concern, but Bret's protective attitude was unexpectedly pleasing. "I live in the Beaches," she said in a feeble voice, her fingers tightening around the snifter she was still holding. "The Upper Beaches. My place is a good half-hour away."

Bret's attention was caught by the incredible softness of her mouth. He had to touch those lips. Placing his glass on the night table, he raised his free hand to rest his fingertips on the nape of her neck. The thumb of his other hand stroked her lower lip, then traced the shape of her mouth. "All the more reason for you to stay," he murmured. "And all the more reason why I won't let you go there by yourself."

Cassie began to wonder just why she was trying to resist his offer. She was sure something valid was holding her back, but it didn't seem to be very important at the moment. "This is blackmail, Mr. Parker," she said shakily, putting up a valiant fight against his persuasiveness and her desire. "You know I don't want to put you to the trouble of seeing me home." But he was too close to her, his touch too warmly seductive, and resistance didn't make sense any longer. She gazed at his mouth, wanting to feel it on hers. "Blackmail," she repeated in a whisper.

Bret forgot he'd promised not to make a pass. This moment didn't seem to count, anyway. Cassie wanted to be kissed as much as he ached to kiss her. Lowering his head, he brushed his mouth over hers, telling himself a man could resist only so much temptation.

Cassie's lips parted as a fleeting taste of mint and cognac tantalized her senses.

Desire raced through Bret in a flash flood that was about to sweep away any obstruction in its path. She wanted him. He wanted her. There was no reason to honor his hands-off vow. Why cheat them both of . . .?

Cheat. The word was like a dam shooting up to stop the torrent and redirect it. Abruptly, passion was transformed to protectiveness.

Bret took Cassie's glass and put it on the night table beside his. Wrapping his arms around her, he enfolded her slender body with infinite tenderness. "I made a promise," he said quietly. "If I break it we'll lose something precious: your trust in me. We're both tired and perhaps a bit dizzy from what's happening to us, and now is no time to play with this particular fire." Feeling her body go rigid, Bret decided he sounded stuffy and egotistical. He hated to leave Cassie with the impression he was unaffected by the kiss. "Please," he said simply. "Stay, Cassie. No strings, no games . . . just a decent rest for both of us. And the relief for me of knowing you're tucked safely away here. Okay?"

Cassie still was stunned by the swiftness of her surrender to him. She'd been dreaming about him, thinking about him almost constantly since the first night they'd met, but she'd expected to show a little more self-control. After all, she truly didn't want to get involved with him. It would be the height of foolishness.

She realized he was waiting for her answer. "You don't really offer much choice, do you?"

"I hope not," Bret answered, trailing kisses over her forehead.

Cassie closed her eyes and drifted with the waves

of pure, sweet sensation. "I guess I'll have to stay," she said at last.

Bret knew the joy washing over him was far out of proportion to the situation: How could he be so thrilled just because a woman had agreed to sleep in his spare room? But he was. He smiled inwardly. The people who'd bought his playboy image would have been amazed.

Tightening his arms around Cassie, he closed his eyes and held her as if to imprint the contours of her body on his own, to warm him through the night. "I'll find you that T-shirt," he said at last. Releasing her, he took his cognac and left the bedroom, downing the drink in one swallow.

Somehow he was able to give Cassie the shirt a few minutes later, say good night, and go to his own room to stay.

Reluctantly alone, Cassie put on the soft cotton shirt that held traces of Bret's fragrance along with its freshly laundered scent. Her eyes misted over as she thought of his tenderness and the tremor she'd felt in his body when he'd held her.

Lying in bed, her lips curved in a smile, prim and proper Cassie Walters was sorely tempted to tiptoe down the hall to the master bedroom to crawl in beside Bret and cuddle close to him while he was asleep and wouldn't know what she was up to.

Instead, she fell asleep herself and dreamed of satiny caresses and tangled limbs and eager mouths.

Bret was awake just before nine, too elated by the knowledge of Cassie's presence to sleep any longer.

An unpleasant thought struck him: What if she'd gotten up at first light to go home?

Pushing back the covers from his naked body, he rose and grabbed a dark blue robe; its color was a pleasant reminder of Cassie's eyes. He was knotting the belt when he remembered he still had her car keys. He hadn't meant to keep them once she'd agreed to stay, but he'd forgotten all about them.

Or perhaps, he mused as he found them in the pocket of his tweed blazer, he hadn't forgotten. Perhaps it was a kind of Freudian slip.

He was content until he recalled something she'd said: "There are taxis, you know."

Quietly, he opened his bedroom door and stepped into the hall, listening for any sound. There was none. He moved toward the spare room, hesitated at the door, and finally opened it carefully to peek in.

Cassie lay just as he'd pictured her, arms hugging a pillow to her breast, breathing deep and even, lips curved in a blissful smile.

He closed the door and wandered to the kitchen to fix himself a mini-breakfast that would tide him over until Cassie was awake.

His brain was fuzzy, though not with exhaustion from the late night. Adrenaline was flowing too fast inside him for weariness. He just couldn't understand the effect Cassie had on him. The sight of her in bed asleep had given him a rush of fondness that made no sense at all. He hardly knew her, yet she was slipping effortlessly into his heart.

When Cassie opened her eyes she was completely disoriented.

There was nothing unusual about her confusion; it even happened in familiar surroundings when she first woke up.

But in the strange room, with only shards of light filtering through closed curtains, she panicked, sprang from the bed toward what she expected to be a door, and slammed into a wall. The impact knocked the wind out of her, causing a groan and a little yelp of pain as her forehead took the brunt of the blow.

Bret flew into the room in time to see her standing by the wall with a bewildered expression, her fingers gingerly rubbing her head, her body swaying slightly. He rushed to her side, steadying her with one hand on her waist while the other gently examined the beginnings of a bump.

Cassie scowled up at him, still trying to sort things out. Gradually she remembered who and where she was. She had no trouble identifying the man hovering over her; hadn't she just been making torrid, abandoned love with him?

His large hand, resting at her waist, was warm and strong; his other hand, at her brow, was soothing. She shivered with renewed excitement. "I'm sorry," Bret said hastily. "Did I hurt you?"

Cassie's heartbeat, already thumping violently from the shock of colliding with a wall, accelerated. She took a deep breath, trying to calm herself. It didn't help. The scent of soap and familiar after-shave on his just-showered body went straight to her head and down to her knees with the effect of overproof liquor.

"You didn't hurt me," she said, wondering if he could hear the tremor in her voice. "I hurt myself. I crashed into your wall." Turning to peer at the point of contact, she added, "I hope I didn't mark it."

Bret chuckled and shook his head. "There are moments, Cassie, when you carry politeness too far. No, you didn't mark the wall, but it's hardly worth considering when it's your head that matters. Let's have a look." Crooking his index finger under her chin he raised her face to check her injury. "You definitely have a little bump coming up there," he said sympathetically. "Should we get you to a doctor? There's always the chance of concussion."

"Heavens, no," Cassie interrupted, then offered a sheepish smile. "I have to admit this isn't the first time I've banged my head that way. I'm not too bright when I first wake up."

"It's my fault," Bret said, realizing the room was in semidarkness. "I should have opened the curtains last night."

"I could've done that myself," Cassie reminded him. "It wouldn't have made any difference. Believe it or not, I've run into walls in my own room. It's embarrassing but true."

Bemused by the thought of the competent, graceful Cassie Walters as a morning klutz, Bret felt another rush of affection, the kind he thought it should have taken years to build between two people.

Brushing back a strand of dark hair that had come loose overnight from her sleek braid, his self-control was eroded by another surge of feeling, one of desire, as he became acutely aware of how enticing Cassie was in his plain white shirt, her breasts high and rounded. He recalled how crisp she looked in her uniform, how he'd considered her somewhat less than voluptuous. How wrong he'd been, he realized.

Her body responded to the slow perusal of his gaze, the tips of her breasts stiffening until they were clearly outlined against the clinging cotton.

His hand, still resting on the top curve of her hip, felt the warmth of her, the ragged rise and fall of her breathing.

Events were conspiring against his rash promise of the night before. But it was a new day, wasn't it? She wasn't tired now. She could make a rational decision. Her desire was as sharp as his own. He was certain of that. Why not . . .?

He looked down at her and lost himself in the dark, uncharted seas of her eyes. Yes, he saw desire. He also saw trust. Vulnerability. "You're sure you're okay?" he asked.

Not exactly, she thought, but she nodded.

There were times when he hated his infernal sense of honor. "I'll go fix us some breakfast, then," he said, moving away from Cassie while he still was able to. At the door, he paused. "I'm no cook, but I can microwave frozen muffins or biscuits. Any preference?"

What Cassie wanted had nothing to do with baked goods. What she wanted had everything to do with the man standing calmly in the doorway looking at her.

Suddenly she remembered how little she was wearing. She grabbed the red terry-cloth robe he'd left for her the night before, and quickly pulled it on to cover herself. Bret Parker certainly wasn't having any trouble turning down what she'd come very close to offering. When was she going to realize that the charm he directed toward her meant nothing? That the kiss that had shattered her was a mere amusement he'd already forgotten? "You don't have to give me breakfast," she mumbled.

"Which do you prefer?" he repeated. She looked so vibrant in the red robe, and so cute. She practically could wrap the thing around her body twice. He wished she'd answer, so he could leave before it was too late. He was a man, not a saint.

Cassie saw his impatience. "Honestly," she started to say. "There's no need—"

"Muffins," Bret decided. "I have cheese and various jams and jellies. It's not a substantial meal, but enough to keep body and soul alive for a while. Would you like juice right away?"

She shook her head. He didn't have to sound so irritable. *He* was the one who'd insisted she stay in his damned apartment. *He* was insisting on giving her breakfast. She was perfectly willing to get out and clear the way for one of his more exciting lady friends.

"Feel free to take a shower," Bret suggested, wondering why he tormented himself this way. Now he wanted to be transformed into a bar of soap.

Cassie nodded, deciding a shower sounded nice. It might cool her off. In jeans and a blue sweat shirt Bret Parker looked too good. He also smelled too good and felt too good. She needed something to douse the fires he'd started within her.

He hesitated, hating to leave her even for a while. Especially with the knowledge that she'd be in the shower—naked, glistening with water streaming over her pale skin, hair loosened from her tight braid . . . "I'll get the coffee started," he said, almost choking out the words. He was gone the next instant.

Cassie looked at herself in the mirror, frowning. She'd never been so confused in her life. Here she was, hurt because he wouldn't give her a tumble, yet he probably was doing her a favor. She didn't play in his league.

Actually, she reminded herself with a deepening scowl, she didn't play in any leagues. When it came to the game of romance, she'd sidelined herself ages ago. Affairs, she'd observed, invariably had unhappy endings. And judging by her own family, marriages didn't fare much better. She'd opted out of the whole sorry mess. Life was safer that way, she'd thought.

She sighed. So much for safety. A simple butlering

assignment had changed everything. Bret Parker, it turned out, wasn't terribly interested even in an affair with Cassie Walters.

Turning her back on her reflection, she headed for the shower. Game over. Game called, she thought. Won . . . or lost—she wasn't sure which —by default.

Four

Dressed again in her black tuxedo pants and white shirt, the top two buttons left undone and the sleeves folded back twice, Cassie tidied the bathroom, putting things away with abrupt, impatient motions.

Bret Parker was *such* a thoughtful host, she fretted silently. The bathroom attached to the spare bedroom lacked for nothing. The night before, when he'd given her his shirt, he'd said she would find whatever else she needed in the vanity, including a disposable toothbrush, but she hadn't realized he supplied scented hair conditioners and facial creams. There was even a selection of fine perfumes, Cassie thought furiously while she rebraided her damp hair. She stuck out her tongue at her reflection as she straightened up. What a starry-eyed dope she'd been.

After quickly applying her makeup she returned to the bedroom to strip off the sheets and fold them, thinking that Bret must keep laundries awfully busy, what with all his lady guests. Well, she should have been grateful she'd come to her senses before anything she would regret had happened. "Men," she muttered. They were charming rascals, every last one of them.

Slipping her bow tie and other belongings into the many pockets of her custom-made tux, she carried the cummerbund and jacket out to the coat rack by the front door, then summoned a cheery little smile and marched out to the kitchen. "Smells wonderful," she said.

Bret was frowning at the coffeepot. "I always make it too strong."

He looked genuinely worried about it, Cassie thought. He probably knew how endearing his fussing was. "I like it strong," she assured him. "Can I help with anything?" She flatly refused to think about how great his lean hips looked in his faded jeans, how inviting his strong arms and chest were, how appealing the little creases in his forehead.

He looked up at her and stared for a long moment.

She grew uncomfortable. What was he thinking? Could he see through her blithe act? "Can I help?" she repeated.

He shook his head. "Just go sit at the table in the solarium. I'll be with you in a minute."

Cassie went to the glass-enclosed balcony and stood looking out at Lake Ontario, its rippling surface dappled with platinum reflections of sunlight.

"Looks as if it'll be a great day, doesn't it?" Bret remarked as he entered the small, cozy room. "I'll bet it's beautiful on the boardwalk over in your end of town."

The boardwalk, Cassie thought. One of her favorite havens. She wondered whether she'd ever passed Bret there; she doubted it. He was the kind of man she'd have noticed.

She turned up the voltage of her smile, at the

same time wondering how many women he'd taken for romantic walks.

Sitting down on one of the white-framed, yellow-upholstered chairs at the matching white table, she had to admire the effort he'd made, putting out jonquil place mats and daisy-sprigged napkins, floral china, a white wicker basket with warmed muffins wrapped in white linen, a cheese plate, and several little pots of preserves.

"This is lovely," she commented carefully, stabbed by jealousy. Everything was perfectly designed for entertaining females. This man had the art of romance down to a science, she decided.

"I like this little room," he answered absently, checking to be sure he'd put everything out. "But it's my sister's doing, not mine. Trish—you remember her? The tall one. Anyway, she's the decorator. She wanted to help put my apartment together, and I let her have her way on the condition she remembered I'm a man."

Cassie reflected that his maleness would be difficult to overlook, but she said nothing.

"Trish did okay," Bret went on, lowering himself into the chair opposite Cassie. "Except for a few touches like the daisy napkins." He raised his glass in a silent toast before drinking half of the juice down in one gulp.

Cassie picked up her own glass and responded to the salute, then took a sip. "Freshly squeezed," she remarked, not surprised. But why was he turning on the charm for her? Force of habit, probably.

"I considered adding champagne," Bret said. "What are those orange juice and champagne things called?"

"Mimosas," Cassie supplied. "It was a nice thought, but I'm glad you didn't. I'm sort of a purist about orange juice. I prefer it straight."

He passed her the basket of muffins. "Somehow I knew you would."

Taking a blueberry muffin, Cassie considered asking why he'd said that. She was well aware that many people thought of her as a prig, and not just because she was a butler. Even as a child she'd been a little Goody-Two-Shoes. Trying so hard not to cause any trouble in her volatile home, she'd turned into a quiet, submissive little angel —on the surface, anyway. Her inner self was another matter.

"Don't get me wrong," she said defensively, returning to the subject of mimosas. "I like champagne. Even cheap bubbly. It's just that plain orange juice—" She stopped abruptly, all at once swept back to her college days, when she hadn't managed to be a rebel, with or without a cause, no matter what her peers thought. She wasn't in college anymore, she realized, and she didn't have to explain herself to Bret Parker.

Nor, to be fair, did he have to explain himself to her. What right had she to be incensed about his busy . . . social life? It was none of her business if he had females coming into his apartment in shifts!

Bret saw her tension and wondered about it. The question of whether or not to put champagne in the orange juice just didn't seem adequate cause. "Have some preserves," he suggested, trying to ease the charged atmosphere. "My mother keeps me supplied."

"Your mother makes jams?" Cassie asked, jumping on the innocuous subject. "I had no idea anyone's mother still did things like that."

"Mine does," Bret said with pride. He got a kick out of his mother. "She also makes bread, grows a vegetable garden, even darns socks. Nobody in the family will wear them, but she gives them to charity. Says she can't abide waste." Bret was chatting idly in the hope of making Cassie relax a bit. Something was bugging her. "I grew up wearing darned socks," he went on. "I can't tell you how much I hated them. They're bumpy, as if you have blisters or calluses, or stones in your shoes."

Cassie couldn't suppress a smile at the mental picture of Bret Parker limping around in darned socks. "Have we just uncovered the true secret of your meteoric rise to the top?" she asked, teasing him.

A breakthrough, Bret decided. Maybe she simply was nervous. "Right," he agreed, following the encouraging line of conversation. "I recall the very day I decided to reach for the brass ring. There was this girl . . . a cheerleader."

"Isn't it always a cheerleader?" Cassie put in dryly, smearing a bit of blueberry jam on part of her muffin.

Bret, cutting Camembert into wedges, stopped and studied her for several seconds. "I'll bet you were never a cheerleader," he said gravely.

Cassie bristled. Was her misfit youth so obvious? He wasn't satisfied to make her feel inadequate as a woman; did he have to attack the girl she'd been as well? "As a matter of fact I wasn't," she admitted, biting hard into the jam-laden muffin. It crumbled all over her plate.

Frowning, Bret wondered how and why his foot had gotten permanently embedded in his mouth. "That was a compliment, Cassie," he said with a gentle smile. "Don't ever tell Karen, though. She was head cheerleader in high school."

"I thought you said you had a crush on a cheerleader," Cassie said, wishing she hadn't revealed her sensitivity.

"I had a crush, yes. But I haven't liked cheerleaders since the night of the last sock hop of my senior year."

Cassie imagined the scene. "When you took off your shoes your cheerleader saw your darned socks. Did she give you a hard time about them?"

Bret nodded sadly. "She also made sure, in her braying, rah-rah voice, that everyone at the dance knew about them. I must admit Mom tends to be creative, of course. The socks were black; the darning yarn was fuchsia. She always tried to make the mending look like a design. It rarely worked."

By this time Cassie was smiling. The man was impossibly winning. "Are you putting me on, Mr. Parker?"

"I am not, Ms. Walters." He finished cutting the cheese and offered her a wedge. "Have some of this?"

She accepted. "I find it hard to believe any girl would laugh at your darned socks—given your other, uh, attributes."

Bret glowed at Cassie's reluctant compliment. "Well, that young lady taught me an important lesson in life."

"What lesson is that?" Cassie asked, drawn into the silly conversation in spite of herself.

"Never let a cheerleader see your darned socks." Bret suddenly grew more serious. "And let me tell you, Cassie, these days I'm surrounded by cheerleader types who are just waiting to see whether I'll show a sock that's been darned."

Cassie was surprised by the edge in his tone. She realized he had insecurities, the same as anyone else. Still new to success, he was afraid someone could take it all away from him. And talk in the media of his so-called "humble origins" bothered him. It was too bad he couldn't just enjoy his victories, she thought. Bret Parker had earned his brass ring many times over.

What really surprised her was that he'd let her glimpse his vulnerable side, and she didn't think it was a ploy to win her sympathy. If anything, he seemed embarrassed by what he'd said.

Bret was even more amazed than Cassie. He didn't like showing his weaknesses, his fears. "Anyway," he went on hastily, deciding to redirect the conversation, "that's why it's a compliment when I say you aren't a cheerleader. What you are is a—"

"A butler," she interrupted. That was all he needed to know. There would be no intimate sharing of life stories, no soul-baring. Not from her, at any rate. She smiled and spoke lightly, teasingly. "Enough about me. Let's talk about something else."

Bret tipped back his head and laughed. He liked Cassie's wry humor. But he intended to learn something about her whether she wanted him to or not. "A butler," he repeated. "That's right. The epitome of quiet discretion. Saying little, listening, and observing all." Warming to his subject, he took a sip of coffee, then smiled at her. "You move through a roomful of people, Cassie, carrying your silver tray like a shield that makes you invisible. Before long you've got everyone pegged. You know who dominates any group, who wants something, who's lying in the reeds waiting to see what goes down."

Cassie choked on her coffee. The man was too much. He'd described exactly the mental games she played when she was around other people. It was a habit she'd developed as a child, from being overshadowed and overwhelmed by the people around her.

Bret leaned forward, patting her back. "I knew the coffee was too strong."

Cassie shook her head. "No, honestly. It's perfect. I was just . . ." She didn't finish. Why admit how right he'd been?

He sat back in his chair and grinned. "It's true, isn't it? You're the fly on the wall. The watcher."

"And you," Cassie shot back, "appear to be the watcher watching the watcher." She frowned as she mentally repeated the statement, wondering if she'd gotten it right.

With a laugh, Bret picked up the pot of orange marmalade and thrust it toward her, for some reason compelled to give her things. "I enjoy watching the watcher," he said quietly. "I'd like to do more of it."

Every fiber of Cassie's body was suddenly leaping to attention. What was he saying?

He leaned forward and touched her wrist, stroking it with his fingertips, weakening her already shaky resolve. "I want to get to know you, Cassie."

She looked out through the wide expanse of window at the blindingly clear azure sky, dotted here and there with a few cloud puffs. She sensed that for her this was an important moment. For him it was probably nothing more than a way to while away a morning. "Why?" she asked at last.

Bret was taken aback. "Why?" He shook his head as if to clear it, then answered her question as sincerely as possible. "Because you're pretty, for starters, and I'm enough of a typical male to be attracted to pretty. Because you're different, and I'm jaded enough to like different. Because," he said very softly, taking her hand in both of his, "there's something magic happening between us, and I'm foolish enough—or wise enough—to believe in magic."

His words hit her hard, but certain images flitted through her mind: Bret Parker, photographed with stunningly beautiful women; Bret Parker's spare bathroom, with its miniature perfume counter. "Are you jaded?" she asked.

He blinked. She'd done it to him again. Studying her, he decided his best defense was her own technique: a question for a question. "What do you mean by the word?"

"Sated," she said immediately. "Had enough of just about everything."

"Then no," he responded slowly, raising her hand to his lips. "I can't be jaded. There are lots of things I haven't had enough of yet."

Cassie was paralyzed for a brief moment, then galvanized into action as she saw clearly that she was in over her head. Yanking her hand away, she gulped down the remainder of her coffee, pushed back her chair, and jumped up. "As they say, so many women, so little time," she blurted out. The instant the words were out she wanted to recall them. She couldn't, so her best bet was to run for it. "Thanks for letting me stay here last night," she said as she raced from the kitchen. "And for breakfast. You're a thoughtful man. Really. 'Bye."

Bret sat perfectly still for several seconds, then realized what was happening and bolted after Cassie, catching up with her as she was grabbing her jacket from the rack by the front door.

Belatedly he realized he was paying for the image he'd stupidly allowed himself to acquire. Cassie thought he really was some kind of playboy. She was partly right . . . but only partly. How could he make her believe that? he wondered frantically.

She was patting her jacket pockets, frowning.

Bret fished her key ring from his jeans pocket. "Is this what you're looking for?"

Reaching for the keys, Cassie was both relieved

and perversely disappointed when he handed them over.

"Thanks again," she mumbled.

"Why are you running?" he asked bluntly.

She was too panicky to think of a polite lie, so she simply told the truth. "Because I feel that magic you were talking about. I don't want to feel it. I refuse to feel it. So . . . good bye." She made a beeline for the door.

Her desperation was contagious. "Wait!" Bret cried as her fingers curled around the doorknob.

Cassie paused. "For what?"

He had to think fast. "Your purse. You're forgetting your purse."

"I didn't have one. I never carry a purse to a job."

He hadn't noticed. "But you're wearing makeup. I know I didn't supply that."

"Along with everything else?" Cassie asked sarcastically, and immediately considered having her tongue cut out. Did she have to be so obvious? What had happened to the Cassie who could hide her feelings so expertly?

Bret frowned, full comprehension dawning slowly. "You were upset by all the stuff in the bathroom?"

"Don't be silly. They were wonderful. Every bachelor should keep honeysuckle-scented body lotion in his medicine cabinet." The tongue would definitely have to go, she decided furiously.

Jealous, Bret thought. She was jealous. It pleased him enormously, but he thought he'd better set her straight on a few things. His mouth turned up in a grin. "Have you forgotten my sisters? They don't live in downtown Toronto. My apartment is a perfect place for them to crash when they hit the city on a shopping spree."

"Look," Cassie protested feebly. "It's none of my affair . . . my business . . . who sleeps with . . . in your apartment or why you have feminine . . . things . . . in your spare bathroom."

"I see it hasn't occurred to you," Bret put in, "that if I had a woman here for more intimate purposes, she'd hardly be staying in the guest room."

Cassie winced, feeling like a fool. As usual her natural wariness and negative attitude had made her jump to conclusions. Nevertheless, she was all the more convinced that she would do well to conquer her crush on Bret Parker. "I already said it's none of my business—"

"Of course it's your business." Bret interrupted again.

She stared at him, taken aback. "It is?"

"In my opinion it is," he said firmly. "I talked about magic between us, and I said I'd like to get to know you; why wouldn't you want to know how many other women hear the same things from me?"

Cassie couldn't resist: "How many?" she asked with a tiny grin.

Bret laughed. "Only you, Cassie." When he saw her roll her eyes in understandable disbelief, he went on hastily. "I don't blame you for jumping to conclusions about me, Cassie. I deserve it. But I'm not the person I'm portrayed as in the media. Not exactly, anyhow. I'm single, and known to hostesses as a man who usually can figure out the right fork to use, and I don't object too strenuously to playing escort to unattached ladies or being an extra man at parties."

Cassie wasn't crazy about hearing what he was saying. "A regular do-gooder, aren't you?" she muttered.

Bret forged ahead. "Some of those ladies happen to be celebrities—thus the pictures and the items in the gossip columns. But there's something you should know, Cassie. One reason I'm asked to play escort is that I'm not in the habit of trying to jump those women's bones. You'd be surprised how many ladies want male companionship without romantic involvement." He paused, then hit her with his zinger. "They don't all respond to me the way you do, Cassie."

Cassie's jaw dropped. "How could you say such a thing?" she said huffily. "And I thought you were such a gentleman."

"You have no idea what a gentleman I've been, Cassandra Walters. But to return to the main issue: I won't claim to be a complete celibate, but I'm not promiscuous—and don't try to deny that's the word you had in mind." Crooking his finger under her chin, he grinned down at her. "I can supply references if you wish," he said quietly.

Cassie had to smile, but the emotions Bret created within her were too strong already, and they were growing in intensity. "You're a lovely man," she said, "but I can't deal with this. With you. Really. I just can't." She twisted the doorknob, telling herself to be strong for a few more seconds. Once out the door she could escape. With a quick tug, she opened it.

Before he could consider the rashness of his action, Bret's hand shot out and pushed the door shut. When Cassie whirled on him, her blue eyes flaring, he dragged her into his arms and lowered his mouth to hers, stifling her protest.

Cassie tried to be outraged, but some part of her was glad he wouldn't let her go. She felt a primitive thrill at finding him strong enough, caring enough, to knock down the barriers of her fears.

At first his kiss was forceful, almost bruising, a statement that he was prepared to crush any resistance. But as Cassie's lips parted and softened, he grew gentle, running his tongue slowly, soothingly around the fleshy inner circle of her mouth, then dipping into the warm sweetness where her tongue met and danced with his.

"Cassie," he whispered, scarcely releasing her lips as he spoke, turning her name into a verbal caress that vibrated between them. His hand moved over her back, molding her body to his while he tasted her honeyed nectar.

Cassie's arms crept upward to twine around his neck. The onslaught of sensation was like a huge breaker catching her with such power, she could only ride its crest and revel in the exhilaration of the adventure. She couldn't think, but it didn't seem to matter, because she didn't want to think. For once, she wanted only to feel.

Her response was everything Bret had been dreaming of since he'd first lost himself in the shimmering desire in her eyes. Stripped of her reserve by his surprise move, she was all throbbing eagerness and soft surrender. He understood now why she was so wary; such intensity of feeling made her even more vulnerable than he'd realized.

The thought was sobering. Had he been too impulsive? He didn't want to hurt her.

It was his turn to panic. Curving his hands over her shoulders, he thrust her away from him. "Is that what scares you, Cassie?"

He knew he sounded almost angry, but couldn't help himself. "Let me tell you a secret," he said with a growl, digging his fingers into her yielding flesh. "It scares the hell out of *me!* I don't want this any more than you do. I hate what you're doing to me. My life was just fine until you walked into it, and now, all of a sudden . . ."

Abruptly releasing her, he turned his back so he couldn't see her troubled expression. "You know why I see so many women? Because there's safety in numbers. Because if I go out with somebody once, twice at the most, I don't get involved, and I don't hurt her or me or anyone. No complications. I like my life that way. Why did you have to toss me this curve? You're looking at a reformed romantic, Cassie. I used to believe in hearts and flowers, but then I discovered the joy of believing in success and power and having a good time."

Cassie was struck by the similarities between Bret's outlook and her own. But he wasn't making much sense. "Then why?" she asked. "Why the kiss? The charm? All of it? Were you checking to be sure you can turn it on any time and with anyone you choose?"

Bret didn't blame her for thinking that way, but it made him angry. He raked his fingers through his hair and spoke in a harsh rasp. "Because, dammit, the only thing that makes me more scared than getting involved with you is letting you escape. Whether I like it or not, woman, I'm already involved with you!"

Cassie was stunned into silence. But Bret didn't notice. Before she could try to speak, he turned and hauled her against the hard wall of his chest, his arms unbreakable bonds around her, his mouth capturing hers in a kiss so demanding and possessive, she knew she'd never really been kissed before in her life.

Her hands fluttered at her sides for a moment, then rested at Bret's waist. Heat emanated from him right through his thick cotton sweat shirt, searing her palms, making her ache to touch his bare skin, to feel the smoothness of him. Reaching under the shirt she felt the leap of his body and heard his gasp of need. His response sent an unfamiliar rush of heady power through her; she pressed herself against him while her lips parted to welcome the sweet invasion.

Bret was dizzy with wanting her. He slipped one hand under her jacket and pressed against the base of her spine.

The heat of him strained against her, making her fleeting sense of power disappear to be replaced by an all-consuming desire. Cassie's body arched against him, her hands greedily exploring the broad planes of his back under his shirt. The overwhelming, unfamiliar need she felt was frightening in its intensity, and she knew with a terrible certainty that if he did make love to her, possessed her even once, her life would be irrevocably altered, and so would she. "This is crazy," she cried, burying her face against his shoulder. "I'm not ready for this, Bret. Please stop. Please make *me* stop!" She knew it wasn't fair for her to beg him to put on the brakes, but she was out of control.

Bret's innate protectiveness conquered his passion. "Okay," he said, struggling to catch his breath and rein in his feelings. He put his arms around Cassie's shoulders and held her, pressing kisses to the throbbing vein in her temple. "Okay, Cassie. We've stopped. It's all right." He kept whispering the soothing words until the sudden conflagration had subsided to embers, then he laughed raggedly. "Hey, we're adults, right? We can take charge of our emotions, can't we?" He wasn't sure whether he was reassuring Cassie or himself.

Carefully, Cassie put her hands on the outside of his shirt. She couldn't calm down as long as she was touching his warm skin. She wondered what was going to happen now. Maybe he would let her go home. She didn't want to leave him, but was sure it would be the smartest thing to do.

"Spend the day with me," he urged. "A walk. A movie. Anything. Will you do that?"

Cassie's nagging little voice of reason said no. Cassie told it to mind its own business. She looked up at Bret and smiled, surrendering to what seemed inevitable. "I'd love to go for a long walk with you," she said softly, then grinned. "One problem, though."

"What problem?" he said. "Whatever it is, we'll solve it."

She laughed. "I'm sure we will. I want to drop in at my apartment, that's all. To change clothes. I'm a little tired of this monkey suit."

Bret grinned and hugged her. A Sunday-afternoon walk with Cassie Walters suddenly promised to be the most exciting thing he'd done in a long, long time.

Five

As Cassie unlocked her apartment door, she realized it was the first time any man except her father had entered her inner sanctum . . . and that particular occasion had turned into a disaster.

She didn't want to think about that awful day. In one unprecedented confrontation she'd been transformed from Daddy's little angel into the family black sheep. She still was trying to get used to her new role. She didn't enjoy it much, but there was no way she was going to back down, to knuckle under to her domineering, hypocritical father's demands, even if he refused to speak to her for *another* ten months. So there, she told him silently . . . and a bit childishly.

As she pushed the door open, she automatically scanned the small room to be sure it was neat, then laughed inwardly at herself. Of course her apartment was neat. It was always neat. She was incapable of having it any other way. All those surprise, militarylike inspections of her room when she was a kid had turned her into a compulsive neatnik.

Actually, she thought, it was sort of comical to

look back on now, but those days, when she'd done all but salute her ex-navy-captain father, had left their mark. At the moment, she had to admit, she was glad. She wouldn't have wanted Bret Parker to think she was sloppy.

"Can I offer you anything?" she asked him politely. "A drink, coffee . . .?" *Me?* she was tempted to add.

"Nothing, thanks," Bret replied, his quick glance taking in his surroundings. He was vaguely troubled by what he saw.

Cassie decided she was too sensitive. Instantly her gaze was following his, and she was worried by his slight frown. What was wrong with her apartment? Had she left something out of place? Had her home been invaded overnight by dust balls?

Maybe the problem was her decor. Bret was accustomed to more luxury than her apartment offered. But what did the man expect from a woman who ran a butler service? Something out of this month's *Apartments Lavish*?

Relax, she told herself. Her home was her home. She was what she was. "I'm a bit of a rolling stone," she heard herself explaining. "So my furniture is the assemble-it-yourself stuff. You know, the kind you buy by driving up to a giant warehouse on a Saturday morning and standing in endless lines so you can carry home a bed frame in a flat box."

Bret chuckled, picturing her doing just that, never dreaming of asking anyone to give her a hand, struggling to drag her furniture up from her car and poring over confusing instructions until she got the pieces put together. From watching her work he could tell she was an independent lady. It was one of the things he liked about her.

But her apartment, her furniture, did bother him. The place said something about her, as her career choice did: Cassie approached life her own way, and that way wasn't particularly traditional. Why the observation bothered him, he wasn't sure. "Nice place," he said truthfully. It was attractive, he had to concede, and suited her. "Cheerful," he added. "But no-nonsense. Like you."

Her eyes widened. No-nonsense? Obviously she had *him* fooled. She smiled. "I won't be long."

Bret smiled back, his mind only half on what she'd said.

After she'd gone into the bedroom he lowered himself into a white leather chair and continued taking in the details around him. The color scheme was black and white, like her Jeeves suit, made lively by cushions in vivid primary colors. There was a glass-topped coffee table, its base four hinged slabs of wood, with several travel books on top. Framed blown-up photographs hung on the walls, beautiful scenes of faraway places. There were no bookshelves.

Odd, he thought. Cassie had struck him as a reader.

Then he noticed a stack of hardcover volumes on a folding end table. Getting up, he went over to check out his suspicion. Sure enough, they were all from the library. The assorted books included two novels, one history of Ireland, one biography, and three travel books.

He was getting the picture. Permanence wasn't for her.

Returning to the chair, he leafed absently through a magazine, which had a travel agency's brochures on Scotland acting as a bookmark in an article about the Hebrides.

Bret tossed the magazine down, recalling that Max had talked once or twice about wanting to buy into the Jeeves Agency, either as a partner or in an outright purchase from Cassie. She hadn't accepted the offer—but neither had she ruled it out, according to Max.

Glancing around her apartment, Bret was struck by the sinking feeling that Cassie could—and just might—decide to fold her tent and silently steal away before he'd even had a chance to know her. The sadness the prospect caused him was startling.

He didn't care for the idea that a woman could have such power over him, but there was no point pretending it wasn't true. He wanted Cassie in a way he'd never wanted any woman—not even Elizabeth Owen.

He'd nearly married Elizabeth two years before, thinking it was time he settled down, reaching the point where he wanted some kids of his own.

One disillusionment later he'd decided settling down was highly overrated, and he'd have to be satisfied to be an uncle, not a father. Marriage wasn't for him.

"All set," Cassie said, returning from her bedroom in what Bret considered record time.

"I should've realized you'd be quick," he remarked with a grin. There was a little tug in the region of his heart as he saw how appealing she was in jeans and an oversized pink sweater. He was seeing a Cassie different from the butler in a tux, though not entirely—she still was sporting her braid. He'd hoped she would undo it; he couldn't tell how long her hair was, whether it was straight or curly, thick or fine. One thing he did know: His preference had suddenly changed from blondes to brunettes.

Cassie smiled, warmed to her toes by the way he was gazing at her. "Why should you have realized I'd be quick?" she asked, finding it both intriguing and disconcerting that he seemed to guess so many small truths about her, as if he'd known her for a very long time.

Bret draped his arm over her shoulders as they walked toward the front door. "Remember, Cassie," he said with a wink as he held the door open for her, "I'm the watcher who watches the watcher, so I've noticed you organizing those parties: There are no wasted actions, no squandered words, no duplicated efforts. You're a human time-and-motion study."

More of her father's hup-two-three training, she thought. "It sounds more like clinical observation than casual watching," she remarked to Bret when she'd locked the door behind them.

"Believe me, Cassandra," he murmured, hugging her to him on the way down the hall to the elevators, "there's nothing casual *or* clinical about the way I watch you."

The boardwalk along the shoreline of Lake Ontario in the resortlike, trendy Beaches neighborhood was alive with locals and visitors basking in the halcyon days of a warm October.

The fragrance of autumn, of ripe fruit and wood smoke and tangy breezes, was in the air. Cassie inhaled deeply. Fall had always been her favorite time of year, but at the moment she was in heaven.

She didn't have to guess why. With his auburn hair ruffled by a playful wind, his golden skin, and rich, brandy-hued eyes, Bret was the ultimate creature of autumn. And he was hers, at least for the afternoon. She was too intoxicated with pleasure to worry about anything else.

Bret, she noted with interest, was as avid a people-watcher as herself. At that moment he was taking in a quietly charming little scene that was unfolding down on the beach, where a man with white hair and a weathered face was patiently giving three youngsters instruction in the art of skipping stones over the water's sparkling surface. "Nice to see," Bret commented as he and Cassie walked on. "The older generation can still teach computer-age kids an important thing or two."

Cassie laughed quietly but felt a flicker of pain. It had been too long since she'd seen her nieces and nephews. As a teenager she'd looked after them so often, she felt as if she'd helped to raise the older ones.

Given the problems with her parents, a visit home would be too overshadowed by tension to be fun for anybody. She did miss those kids, though. Talking to them on the phone wasn't the same as seeing them, hugging them, looking at their report cards, and watching their faces as they chattered her ear off. If only that one terrible row with her father hadn't turned so bitter, she thought. If only she could explain things to her mother . . . but that was unthinkable. If only there were some other way . . .

"A loony for your thoughts," Bret said, playfully flipping a newly minted Canadian dollar coin engraved with a northern loon.

"Inflation hits everywhere," Cassie responded with a chuckle, and quickly searched for a distraction. She didn't want to spoil the day by talking or even thinking about her problems. "Look," she said, pointing to a line of exotically decorated kites that danced like barnstormers of the 1920s against the clear sky. "Isn't that pretty?"

Her ploy worked. Bret watched in fascination as the kites suddenly swooped down to buzz a startled cluster of gossiping ducks, then zoomed back up with showy loop-the-loops and figure eights. "It's fantastic," he murmured. "Who's doing it?"

"Just some hobbyist, I think," Cassie answered. "He's here most weekends."

Bret turned to smile at her. "At the risk of sounding like a singles' bar swinger," he said as he deftly avoided being caught in the leash of a hyper-active terrier, "do you come here often?"

"As often as I can manage," Cassie said. "I love the water, the sand, the way you can see a whole expanse of blue without some steel-and-glass, geometric skyline getting in the way. It reminds me a little of home."

"Where's home?"

Her eyes glinted with fun. "I wouldn't expect a cloistered Torontonian like you to have heard of it. I'm originally from one of those blink-and-you'll-miss-it towns several hundred miles north of here. My family lives in a real city now, but still up north." Cassie was instinctively avoiding the name of the city, not wanting Bret to make the connection between it and her last name. Her father wasn't famous, but he was fairly well known on a national level because of his political clout. She'd worked hard to become Cassie Walters instead of Fred's little girl, and she wanted to stay that way for a while longer. "Both places are the kind you decide to live in forever or escape from early," she went on, relieved when Bret remained silent. "I escaped. But sometimes I do miss the clean air and open spaces."

"Open spaces?" Bret shot back. "The north? It's covered with dense forests, isn't it?" He was deliberately exaggerating the tenderfoot city-boy role a little, just to tease her.

"That's still open space," Cassie said with a laugh. "At least you don't have to fight crowds of people."

"Just crowds of trees," he retorted. "And black flies."

"Spoken like a true native of the urban jungle," Cassie answered, enjoying the banter. Bret, she'd discovered, was easy to be with. Fun.

"And how do you know I'm a native of this city?" he asked very casually.

A stupid slip, Cassie thought. Why hadn't she ever learned to play male-female games, to feign nonchalant disinterest? "I imagine everyone in Toronto knows you're a native son," she said at last, deciding it sounded logical enough. She couldn't be the only person who'd devoured every syllable written about Bret Parker, could she?

Bret felt ten feet tall, knowing she'd taken the trouble to read about him. On the other hand, he wasn't too thrilled with the impression she must have formed of him. The media really played up the rich-bachelor angle, and he'd never minded before.

As his only line of defense, he chose to treat the whole thing lightly, and he was happily aware of his ability to make Cassie forget what was on her mind by arousing her desire. Bending so his lips grazed her ear, he whispered softly. "It might surprise you to know, Cassie, that there are people in this world—even in this city—who don't know or care who Bret Parker is."

Lovely little thrills rippled through Cassie as Bret's warm breath fanned her skin. Tilting back her head, she closed her eyes to enjoy the sensation.

Bret realized his teasing had backfired. Cassie's response to him was so guileless, and she was so unconsciously, totally sensual, she kept catching him off guard. All of a sudden he found himself fighting an embarrassing arousal.

"Have dinner with me," he blurted out when he and Cassie had resumed their walking.

Her dark brows arched questioningly. "When?"

"Tonight, of course. Well, not just tonight. Other nights too. But tonight for starters."

Boyish, Cassie thought; who'd have expected the famous Bret Parker to be so boyish? "I'd like that," she answered, ignoring the familiar voice inside her when it tried to tell her she was getting more involved than she should. "Remember your charted-out life plans," it nagged. "Think of all the traveling you still haven't done. Think how content you are with your life just as it is. Falling for any man will mess up everything."

Cassie simply refused to listen. She was having too wonderful a time to be practical.

Bret took her to a new Cajun restaurant, where the two of them discovered a mutual passion for spicy food and Louisiana fiddle music.

"Wonderful," Cassie said as she took a bite of blackened red snapper. As always when her senses were delighted, she closed her eyes to savor the experience more acutely.

Bret watched, savoring Cassie, deciding she was by far the most delicious morsel in front of him.

"This is such a great restaurant," Cassie said, glancing at the various dishes being served at the other tables. "I wish I could try everything!"

"Be my guest," Bret offered, telling himself he was referring only to the menu.

Cassie laughed. "Tempting," she admitted. "But I'm already getting full, and I want to leave room for dessert. Something decadent. All those butlering jobs during the flu epidemic mean I can forget dieting for a while."

"A long while," Bret remarked. "You don't need to lose weight. You're perfect."

She grinned. "You know something I do like about men?"

Bret tripped her up on her phrasing. "Something you *do* like? It sounds as if there's a lot you *don't* like about us."

Cassie's eyebrows shot up in surprise. Was that what she really meant? It was hard to think so when she was across from a man who delighted her in every way. She decided to avoid any discussion on the subject. "Anyhow, what I like is that the male definition of *perfect* seems to allow a lot of leeway. I read about a recent study, in fact, that stated while we women look at ourselves and see a collection of flaws, you fellows look at us and zero in on the parts you like. Isn't that nice? If it's true, that is. Do you think it is?"

Bret grinned. "Why do I get the feeling I could find myself in trouble here? You're dealing with a man who grew up with sisters, Cassie. I can usually spot a female's loaded question."

"Why loaded?" she asked, genuinely puzzled. She'd merely been making small talk.

"If I say I believe that study was an accurate portrayal of the typical male's response to women," he explained, his lips forming a smile, "I'll sound like a lech. But if I discount the theory, I'm suggesting we men expect centerfold perfection in women."

"So what's your answer?" Cassie asked, persistent.

He stroked his chin as if thinking the matter over very carefully, then shook his head. "I can't answer," he said at last. "Not when I'm looking at a woman without a single imperfection that I can see, a woman who is so much more than the sum of her parts."

Cassie laughed delightedly. "Wonderful! You ought to join the diplomatic service. They could use you. That was one of the best verbal sidesteps I've heard since the last federal election!"

"I'll take that remark as a real tribute," Bret shot back. "Considering it comes from an expert."

"What? Me?" Cassie said with feigned innocence. She was fully aware of her well-developed talent for muddying the conversational waters.

"It's okay, Cassie. I understand. You have something to hide. Maybe your past includes a stint as a KGB spy or a career as an international jewel thief, and far be it from me to hold it against you."

"Are you suggesting I'm secretive?" Cassie asked with a tiny grin and a silver twinkle in her blue eyes.

Bret wagged his head from side to side. "Such a thought never entered my mind."

Cassie surprised him—and herself—by asking, "What would you like to know?"

"Everything," he blurted out, then realized he might be expecting a bit much on what was, in effect, a first date. "But let's start with the basics. How does a little girl from the northern wilderness end up running Toronto's most phenomenally successful butler agency and party service?"

"By accident," she answered, then took a sip of wine.

She went on. "After graduating from college I kicked around Europe for a couple of years. I supported myself and financed my travels with odd jobs."

"What kind of odd jobs?"

Cassie grinned. "Jewel theft, a bit of espionage . . ."

He narrowed his eyes dangerously.

"Okay, okay. The truth. Let's see: I harvested grapes in the Loire Valley, in France. . . ."

"I do know where the Loire Valley is," Bret said.

"Sorry. I didn't mean to sound like a know-it-all," Cassie said, frowning at her gaffe.

"I was teasing, Cassie." Bret reached across the table to place his hand over hers. "Go on, okay?"

His touch had scattered her thoughts. "Um . . . where was I?"

"In the Loire Valley harvesting grapes."

"Oh. Right. Well, I taught English to the children in a wealthy family in northern Italy."

"You're good with kids, aren't you?" Bret commented, thinking of the way Slugger had warmed to her. "And you're crazy about them."

Cassie wasn't about to admit such a thing aloud; it might start her biological clock ticking again, and she'd decided that particular clock could just wind right down. She had no intention of becoming a mother. In her opinion children ought to have two parents, and since she couldn't imagine herself in a happy marriage . . . "Me?" she said to Bret. "I can't stand the little ankle-biters."

Bret burst out laughing, not believing her for a second. It was a clear case of protesting too much. But he saw no point in belaboring the subject. "What was next in the Cassie Walters saga?"

"After the governess position I turned bartender —sometimes waitress but usually bartender. I must've worked in half a dozen pubs throughout the British Isles. It was great. Then, in London, I read about a course for butlers, and pretty soon I had myself a career."

"How did you manage the work permits?" Bret asked.

Cassie didn't want to say it was because her father had been born in England. She still hoped to skip over her father's identity. "British parentage," she said at last. "So I can work in Common Market countries, or whatever they call them these days." She smiled brightly. "I don't want to talk about myself any more. I'm getting bored with it."

"One more question," Bret insisted. "Would you

want to do all that traveling again? Long-term, that is."

Cassie considered the matter for a moment. "I've given it a lot of thought," she admitted. "The truth is, I had never intended the agency to be my life's work."

To Bret's frustration, the waiter chose that moment to arrive with the dessert menu, and Cassie's attention shifted to the more immediate matter of whether to order the pecan pie, raspberry ice, or peach tart. Bret couldn't get the conversation back to his vital question, so he had no idea whether or not Cassie was thinking seriously about accepting Max's offer and hitting the road again. With every passing moment he knew with greater certainty and urgency just how much he cared about her answer.

Summoning all his restraint, Bret gave Cassie a chaste kiss at her door, hesitated, then left. He wondered whether he'd made a mistake. There was something he'd wanted to tell Cassie, something he should have mentioned. But how could he, without sounding presumptuous?

Cassie was disappointed to find herself alone at home. Bret could have at least *tried* to seduce her, she thought, all her doubts about her attractiveness flooding back.

The nagging little voice inside her head waited until she was lying in bed, then pounced on her fears. "Just as well *he* had some sense," it chided. "You do know you're flirting with disaster, don't you?"

"Oh, shut up," Cassie said aloud, rolling over and pulling the blankets up around her ears. Defiantly, she allowed her favorite Bret Parker fantasies to unfold until she drifted off to sleep and turned them into the sweetest of dreams.

Bret called Cassie on Monday. They had a warm but slightly awkward chat, full of overly polite thanks for the lovely day they'd spent together. Although he tried again to tell her what was on his mind, he couldn't ease into the matter gracefully. If only he'd been seeing her for a longer time, he could simply have explained that before meeting her he'd made some commitments for the week, but from then on he was off the bachelor market until further notice. Yet how could he say it without sounding as if he figured she had nothing better to do than worry about whether he was being unfaithful to her?

Strangely, that was exactly how he felt—that he was about to be unfaithful to Cassie.

Maybe he'd be lucky, he told himself. Maybe there'd be no publicity.

He thought about the lady he'd promised to escort to a party that Tuesday night—an opening-night party for a new Broadway show beginning its Toronto tryout run—the Broadway show of which his date was the star.

No publicity?

Fat chance.

Six

Jan planted herself in front of Cassie's desk and tossed down a yellow telephone-message slip. "Okay, Cass," she said, her expression determined, "the jig's up."

Cassie dragged her attention from the computer screen where she was updating client files, though in truth, her attention wasn't properly focused on the job at hand anyway. With her thoughts constantly straying to the previous Sunday, her perfect Sunday with Bret, it was difficult to become absorbed in the task of filling in details of recent parties Jeeves had organized.

She smiled quizzically at Jan. "What jig? Why do you look so fierce?"

"Because I cannot, will not tell Bret Parker one more time that you're unavailable. Got that? No more."

Cassie shifted uncomfortably in her chair. "I asked you to hold *all* calls, Jan, not just his."

"For the first time since I started working for you two years ago, yes, you did tell me to hold all calls." Jan plunked her leather-mini-skirted bottom in the chair opposite Cassie. "An odd request, to say the least, coming from the woman who's known to be an accessible executive. Just as odd as when our star client, always so good about giving us advance notice for his parties, suddenly needed the service for two last-minute things while Max Webster was sick and Cassie Walters was filling in. Believe it or not, I also started to find it odd that Bret Parker was phoning and phoning and phoning and insisting he had to talk to Cassie, and Cassie wasn't returning his calls. I don't know, call me overly suspicious, but I smell a rat."

"He's *not* a rat," Cassie shot back without thinking, then buried her face in her hands to hide the sudden flaming of her cheeks. "You're right," she admitted. "The jig's up."

Jan stared at her boss in utter amazement. "No," Jan murmured. "He's not a rat. And you've got it bad."

Lowering her hands and facing Jan, Cassie nodded. "Isn't it awful? I know better, Jan. You don't have to tell me how unprofessional I'm being."

"The word *unprofessional* wasn't exactly what I had in mind," she said. "Crazy, maybe. That fabulous hunk of male is pursuing you, and you're not letting yourself get caught?"

Cassie jumped up and walked across the room to the coffee maker. "Want some?" she asked Jan, holding up the pot.

Jan nodded. Cassie filled two cups and handed one to her, then began pacing the room, sipping her coffee.

"Bret Parker?" Jan said aloud. "The man's the catch of the year. The decade. Maybe the century."

"The man just isn't for me," Cassie said with a small groan. "He'd . . . he'd chew me up and spit me out."

Jan shrugged. "I can think of worse ways to go, Cass."

Cassie's lips curved in a tiny smile. She wasn't used to talking things out with another woman. She'd never been one to have girlfriends to confide in; maybe, she thought as Jan's comment made her see a glimmer of humor in this situation, she'd been missing something. "I'm not sophisticated enough for Bret Parker," she said. "Not . . . casual enough."

Jan smiled in sympathy. "Could this have something to do with the picture in the paper of him and that stunning Broadway babe?"

"Not really." Cassie gave an eloquent little shrug of her slim shoulders. "That picture just made me face facts, Jan. The man is big time, main event, a pro of the first order. I knew it all along, but I kept kidding myself. At best I can hope to be a minor flirtation for him. A . . . a sparring partner for a heavyweight champion. I don't want to be a sparring partner. You can get just as hurt, but you hardly ever get a shot at the title."

Jan's jaw dropped. "Main events? Sparring partners? Title shots? What kind of talk is that?"

"I used to watch the fights on television with my father," Cassie mumbled, staring into the depths of her coffee as if to find comfort there.

"You watched the fights?"

"And baseball, hockey, football—"

"I didn't realize you were so close to your father."

"We're not close. We're not even speaking. Haven't been for months." Cassie went to stare out the window, then whirled on Jan. "And that's exactly why I can't get involved with Bret Parker!" She sat down, worrying at her lower lip.

"Wait a minute," Jan said, scratching her head. "Let me get this straight. You're not speaking to Bret Parker because you're not speaking to your father? What does one situation have to do with the other?"

"Everything! Men like my father and Bret Parker are like navy destroyers. They see a prey and they go after it just for the sport, to test their prowess. It's damn the torpedoes, full speed ahead. I don't want to be torpedoed."

"You're such a romantic, Cassie," Jan said teasingly. "First it's sparring partners, now torpedoes? Liz Barrett Browning, eat your heart out."

Cassie laughed aloud. "I've never done this before," she remarked, suddenly feeling much closer to Jan.

"What are you talking about now?"

"About friendship. Confiding in someone. Trust. It's . . . it's kind of beautiful, don't you think?" Cassie said shyly.

Jan sat back in her chair and stared at her boss. "You know, not long ago if someone had asked me to name the sanest person I'd ever met, I'd have said Cassie Walters, without a second's hesitation. And I'd have been wrong. You're a fruitcake!"

Cassie laughed again. "Maybe so, but this fruitcake isn't going to get herself—"

"I know, I know. Chewed up and—Lord, I hate that expression. Now, about Bret Parker. Why not quit being such a coward and just go for it? Anybody with eyes can see you're already suffering over him, so it seems a waste not to have the fun that goes with it."

"Faulty logic," Cassie said seriously. "There are degrees of suffering. I have a low pain threshold, and I've already reached it."

Jan rose. "Okay, Cass. I'll keep fielding the poor guy's calls if you insist. But let me give you a bit of advice: A ship that stays in the harbor might be safe, but ships weren't built to stay in harbors."

Cassie giggled. "First, you got that off a poster. Gift-shop philosophy. Second, somebody probably said that to the captain of the *Titanic*. Third, I get seasick."

Grinning, Jan took her leave.

"Hey," Cassie called after her.

The younger woman paused. "Yes?"

"I forgot to mention how terrific you look with auburn hair."

But who didn't? Cassie thought with a sigh.

The impossible had happened, Bret realized. He was mad at Cassie Walters—damned good and mad.

Thinking about her midnight-blue eyes, so soft and vulnerable, her full, eager lips, that fragile body, he couldn't imagine being angry with sweet Cassie for any reason.

But he wanted to strangle her.

When he got her answering machine on Saturday morning, he slammed down the phone in total frustration.

Okay, he decided. If Cassie wanted him out of her life, he was out of it. Why should he keep trying to get through to the woman? He almost could see her sitting beside the infernal machine, listening to him, choosing not to answer.

His stomach went into a tighter knot every time he heard her low, lovely, recorded voice. "Hello, this is Cassie Walters. I'm not home right now, but . . ."

In a pig's eye she wasn't home.

She was being totally unreasonable by not giving him a chance to explain about the stupid picture in the newspaper. Who did she think she was, anyway? They'd shared one Sunday stroll, one dinner, and she figured she owned him?

His own words came back to haunt him. He'd told her she had a perfect right to know whether he was romancing other women. *He* was no play-boy. Mr. Sincere.

It didn't matter. She could have let him explain.

The lady wasn't interested, he told himself, pacing his apartment like a caged tiger. She was trying to tell him so in her own infuriating way. Wasn't it time he caught on?

It would rain loonies before he tried to contact that woman again.

The following Friday, when he'd been handed loonies in change for the first three purchases he made, he decided he'd been given a sign. He was supposed to try once more to reach Cassie. It was a decree of fate.

But he wouldn't, he decided, try to reach her by telephone.

"Why are you braiding your hair all the time?" Jan asked.

Cassie was standing in her assistant's office, deciding whether or not to go home to her empty little apartment, the one that, in what seemed like a former life, she'd regarded as a haven of solitude. Maybe, she thought, she ought to stick around and do some work. Except that she was caught up on all her work, thanks to the nights she'd chosen to spend at her desk.

She scowled, trying to concentrate on Jan's question. Patting her head as if to check how her hair was styled, she realized the girl was right. The braid was in place. "Stormy weather," she explained.

"Since that guy and you ain't together," Jan crooned.

As usual, Jan made Cassie laugh. "You're a tonic, you know that?"

"And you're kidding yourself about the hairdo. This is the first rainy day all week. My guess is your braid is a reflection of the inner you," Jan remarked. "Up-tight. If you won't smarten up and give that gorgeous guy a call, why don't you go away somewhere?"

Cassie shot her a look of dismay. "Have I been inflicting my lousy mood on you?"

"Heaven forbid," Jan replied in a teasing tone. "Cassie Walters allowing her personal feelings to spill over into her professional life? No, Cass. It's just that I can't take much more of your phony good cheer. All this bravery and pride. Go find yourself a beach and soak up some sun. Take a cruise and have a shipboard romance with some guy, and discard him afterward as if he were a defeated sparring partner."

"I don't think I could do that to anyone," Cassie said softly, actually giving the idea some consideration.

The younger woman shook her head and laughed. "You're hopeless. Want to take in a movie tonight?"

"I thought you had a date."

"No reason you couldn't come along. I'll even let you steal the guy if you promise to give him back. He's not the love of my life but he's okay."

Cassie's eyes widened in shock. "You don't mean that!"

"No," Jan said. "Lay a hand on him and I'll cut it off. But I knew you'd refuse so I figured I might as well sound expansively generous, sophisticated . . ."

Cassie picked up an eraser and threw it at the girl, but she had to concede privately that the silliness had cheered her up.

"I did mean it about the movie, though," Jan added.

"Thanks," Cassie said. "But I think I'll pick up

a video to watch on my new VCR. Something old. A comedy, maybe."

"Sounds good. Try a Cary Grant film."

Cassie wasn't interested in Cary Grant or any romantic hero. "Groucho Marx," she said. *"Duck Soup* will be perfect."

"Sounds like a Friday night to end all Friday nights."

Cassie wished she *could* end all Friday nights, at least for herself. The previous weekend had been rotten. She'd had too much time to think. Hearing Bret's increasingly irritated voice on her answering machine hadn't lightened her mood. She gave a little shiver. "I'm on my way. You sure you don't mind locking up?"

"I'm being met here, so I have to wait around anyway. Get a jump on the traffic, Cass. Leave now. And think about what I said. You're due for a vacation. You need it, you can afford it, you deserve it."

Cassie grinned. "You're reaching me, Jan. I'll go through my collection of travel brochures as soon as I get home, all right?"

Exhausted by the time she wheeled into the driveway of her apartment building, Cassie decided a Groucho Marx movie would undoubtedly be an effective antidote to her uncharacteristically bad mood. A video store was just around the corner, so she could pick up the movie right away. Suddenly her heart leaped into her throat.

There was a red Porsche in the visitor's area.

Cassie checked the license plate. Dear heaven, she realized, it was Bret's car, but he wasn't in it. Was the man seeing *another* woman in her building? Every inch of her body began trembling. It was all she could do to use her coded entry card to let herself into the underground garage and park her car without smashing into a concrete pillar.

As she marched across the garage floor, her high heels clicked in a fast staccato that strengthened her backbone the way a martial drum sends soldiers into battle.

Bret was waiting in the lobby.

Bret's anger disappeared as soon as he saw her. In a beige trench coat, the cowl neck of a black sweater framing her pale face, her long legs shapely in dark stockings, she was all the woman he could ever want, and more.

She looked as if she were a startled doe about to bolt into the depths of the forest, her eyes huge, her expression frightened. How the hell could he stay mad at this creature? She melted his heart. "Hi," he said quietly.

She swallowed hard. He was too gorgeous. His Burberry raincoat hung open over a camel blazer, brown pants, and a casual shirt; she could have sworn he was bathed in a bronze light, and his eyes flickered with coppery flames that still dominated her dreams. It wasn't fair. Staying away from him had been the right decision, she thought, but he was supposed to cooperate. He was supposed to stay away from her too.

Somehow, though a consuming heat was burning inside her, she managed to speak with coolness. "What brings you here?"

Bret saw through her act. He'd been nervous, waiting for her, wondering whether he'd jumped to conclusions about her feelings for him, wondering if he was going to make a complete fool of himself. But her eyes told him everything he needed to know, and his nervousness vanished.

Cassie's days as an independent loner, a free-spirited nomad with no ties to hold her, he decided on the spot, were numbered.

Then he smiled. His *own* days as an independent loner were also numbered, it seemed. "We have to talk," he told her.

Seven

Cassie was acutely conscious of the security man in the glassed-in cubicle to one side of the lobby. "Talk?" she asked Bret in a low voice, determined to control her emotions, trying not to be overjoyed that he cared for her enough to be there, to *want* to talk. Nothing really had changed. They were the same two people she'd already decided didn't belong together.

Bret noticed the way her glance kept darting to the security guard; she hated an audience, he realized. She was also very agitated, an encouraging sign. If attraction had turned to indifference she wouldn't be so tense. Deciding to use her self-consciousness and her taut nerves to his advantage, he made a completely irrelevant remark. "You're carrying a purse," he said, hoping the comment would put her off guard.

It did. "No pockets," she answered, wondering why on earth he'd brought up something so inane. But she went on to explain anyway. "Knit dresses won't even hold miniature compacts, let alone wallets and combs and—"

"So that was the secret of the mystery makeup,"

he commented with a grin. "Special pockets in your tux."

Cassie scowled in puzzlement, then recalled his curiosity about her made-up face that fateful Sunday morning at his place after she'd so foolishly let him talk her into staying there. She was impressed by his memory of such a small detail.

"You look pretty," he said, meaning it. "Elegant. Classy."

"Mmm," she responded, refusing to soften, trying on a flip attitude for size. "Classy Cassie, that's me."

"I've never seen you without your braid."

Her scowl deepened. What was it with people and her braid? First Jan, now Bret. "Look," she said briskly, "we really have nothing to talk about." She made the mistake of looking at him, into his sienna eyes, and she forgot what she was trying to say.

"I thought we were friends," Bret said gently.

"Let's not kid ourselves or each other," she argued in a half-whisper, still sharply aware of their one-man audience. "This isn't friendship. It's just . . . attraction, and it's better left alone."

The security guard suddenly stood up, walked out of his cubicle, and locked it, then nodded briefly at Bret and Cassie. "Time to do my rounds," he muttered.

Oh, no, she thought, now feeling slightly abandoned by the man. Having an audience seemed preferable to being left alone with Bret Parker.

Bret pressed his advantage. "Do we talk in your apartment," he insisted, "or do we go somewhere else?"

Her chin lifted. Fight, her inner voice urged. Don't give in to this insanity. "Neither. I'm going up to my apartment, and you can go . . . somewhere else." To give herself strength, she concentrated hard on the memory of a particular photograph in Wednesday's newspaper.

"Okay," Bret said with a small grin. "You go up to your apartment, then I'll stand in the hall pounding on your door and shouting that you can't hide our baby from me forever, and then you'll let me in because you can't abide a scene . . . and then we'll talk. Or we could skip all that embarrassing business and—"

"Let's go for a walk," Cassie said hastily, certain Bret would carry out his threat.

"A drive," he amended, opening the lobby door and standing aside while Cassie walked out ahead of him. "I'm tired, you're tired, rain's threatening. Besides, those shoes of yours aren't designed for long walks."

Cassie was wary of putting herself in his hands by climbing into his car. "What if I insist on walking?"

"Well," Bret said with a cheerful smile, "let's see. I guess I'd have to pick you up and place you in the car, at which point you'd probably cry for help, the security guard would call the police, and you'd be rescued. I'd be arrested, of course, and the news would be big in the media—"

"Or," Cassie interrupted, rolling her eyes in resignation, "we could skip all that embarrassment."

"Exactly," Bret said with a smug smile, though inwardly he was anything but smug. Cassie was going to put up quite a battle.

"Your timing is a little off," she remarked once she was belted into the passenger seat of his Porsche. "Friday-evening traffic isn't exactly suited to conversation."

"Then just relax while I take us somewhere that is," Bret replied pleasantly.

Neither of them spoke again until he pulled into a parking lot at the foot of the high, sheer cliffs called the Scarborough Bluffs.

"Now, isn't this peaceful?" Bret said, turning to smile at Cassie as he undid his seat belt.

She looked at the wall of clay that rose straight out of the water, a formation dramatically different from the rest of the lake's shoreline. "I've never been here before," she said quietly. "I've heard of the Bluffs, but for some reason haven't gotten around to visiting them."

Bret was certain he knew the reason: Cassie's dreams were of foreign, exotic places, not of pleasures close at hand. He'd spent a lot of late-night hours thinking about her obvious wanderlust, and he couldn't help wondering if she was running from, rather than to, something. "Stick with me," he said with a wink. "I'm a Toronto native, remember? I'll give you a proper tour of my town."

Cassie's battle was becoming more difficult. Bret Parker as a tour guide was a tempting thought. In the closeness of the car she kept getting tantalizing whiffs of his unique fragrance, clean and spicy and male. And each time he spoke his voice resonated around and through her like a touch. "Nice car," she mumbled, clasping her hands in her lap.

Bret raised one brow in surprise. "I didn't think you'd noticed."

"Why? Because I didn't go into raptures over it?" She'd grown up around the various kinds of status cars men worshiped as icons of success. "I've never understood the male fascination with vehicles."

"Neither have I," Bret said honestly. "This car is just part of the image I've cultivated, perhaps foolishly. But, Cassie, if you know anything about me, you know I come from what the media love to call 'working-class origins,' with the implication that there's something wrong with it." He shook his head in disgust. "Well, maybe there is. I have an M.B.A., but because of my supposedly humble background, I found a lot of corporate doors closed to me. It came as quite a shock that the so-called Establishment doesn't like outsiders and upstarts—which I've been called more than once. I take it as a compliment now." Scowling, Bret wondered how he'd launched into his monologue. His early frustrations weren't what he'd meant to talk over with Cassie.

But she softened to his vulnerable side as she never could to total invincibility. "You should," she said gently. "You should definitely consider the word *upstart* a compliment. What you've accomplished in a few short years is amazing, and I'm sure it scares those men behind the closed doors. You undermine their self-importance a little."

Bret felt small pockets of residual anger inside him begin to dissipate as if by magic. Cassie's magic. He found he liked her admiration. "It was all for the best," he went on. "Those closed doors made me mad enough to prove myself, if only for spite." Finally he remembered the original point he'd meant to make. "But you see, when I first saw a way to carve out my own corporate niche, I understood too well that hard work and determination were important, but not enough to put me where I wanted to be. I needed financing, and I got it from maverick businessmen. Those characters tend to be flashy, and that's what they're attracted to, so I learned to fake it. Eventually the old-boy networks behind the closed doors didn't matter. I don't really need the flash now, but it's gotten to be a habit."

Cassie didn't know why he was so self-conscious

about his "flash." There was nothing wrong with red Porsches or good clothes or a glamorous, high-flying lifestyle, especially when Bret had earned the right to enjoy all of it. If she seemed negative it was only because she couldn't see herself competing with all that excitement, couldn't imagine keeping his interest for very long. And, much to her dismay, she deeply wanted to keep Bret Parker's interest for a very long time.

Bret mistook Cassie's pensive expression for disapproval. "Okay," he conceded shortly. Couldn't he make her understand? "Okay, you're right. The stupid car is a statement. Probably a hell of a superficial one. It says I've made it. I can afford it. And it's red—a blatant, look-at-me color. Now you know. I have clay feet. So do those Bluffs you keep staring at, but you seem to find *them* interesting. Look at me, will you!"

Shocked by his outburst, Cassie's gaze darkened to an unfathomable indigo. She had no idea what to say.

Bret was even more stunned than Cassie. He started to laugh. "We're quite the pair, aren't we? There must be something exciting happening between us, because it's making us crazy! I promise you, Cassie, I'm not usually so quick-tempered. But part of it is because trying to read you is like grabbing smoke." Softening his tone, he added, "Talk to me, won't you? Say what you're thinking. It matters a lot."

Cassie couldn't speak. She had a lump in her throat from wanting to take Bret in her arms and tell him every thought that had ever crossed her mind if it would make him happy. She wanted to say his car was wonderful and he was wonderful and even his craziness was wonderful.

But she'd didn't know how or where to start. The habit of masking her feelings had been part of her for too long, and she just couldn't seem to open her mouth and speak.

"Where do you go, Cassie?" Bret asked softly.

"Go?" she repeated in a small voice.

"When you close in on yourself. When your eyes get that faraway look."

"I haven't gone anywhere," she said with total honesty. She was with him more than he could know. "I'm . . . I'm right here, trying to figure out what this is all about."

"It's about so many things," he murmured, stretching his arm over the back of the seat and catching a wispy tendril of blue-black hair that was curled over the nape of Cassie's neck. He wound the silken strand around one finger and found himself warmed by even that much contact with her.

"Mostly," he added, "it's about two dopes letting something pretty special slip away from them. I've been burned, Cassie, and I've been fooled more than once. So I'm leery, but not leery enough. I can't let you walk away. Or I won't. It amounts to the same thing."

She couldn't deny how much she wanted to believe him, to think they really did have a chance together. But he was worldly and strong and larger than life, and she'd spent years trying to become something more than a shadow overwhelmed by other larger-than-life people. "You know my name-sake's fate?" she asked, trying not to let desire cloud her thinking as his fingers grazed the sensitive skin of her neck.

Bret smiled, bemused by the unexpected question. "You mean the Trojan Cassandra?"

She nodded and took a deep, shaky breath. "She tried to warn the city about that wooden horse outside the gates. Nobody listened. Cassandra knew there was trouble ahead, but everyone preferred to believe in happy endings. So they were all doomed. Including Cassandra."

"That's true," Bret said, searching his memory of classic legends, glad he'd been especially interested in them. "Cassandra was blessed with the gift of prophecy and then cursed with the disbelief of the people."

"Just goes to show you," Cassie said with a forced smile. "People should pay attention to a Cassandra's fears."

"Ah, but you've left out something," Bret reminded her. "The whole mess happened because she got her powers from Apollo but wouldn't return his love, so he cursed her. Just goes to show you: A Cassandra's resistance is a big mistake."

She couldn't suppress a smile. "An Apollo is awfully hard to resist," she admitted softly.

"Then don't," Bret urged. He moved nearer to her, as near as possible despite his car's bucket seats and floor-mounted gearshift. Brushing his fingers upward along the right side of her slender throat, he traced the curve of her ear, then her jawline, touching her with just enough pressure to make her face him. "Don't resist, Cassie."

She watched him come closer and closer, as if in slow motion, and when his mouth finally touched hers, his left hand exploring the exposed column of her throat, she closed her eyes in surrender. The kiss was excruciatingly tentative, a contact so light, so brief, she could almost wonder whether it had actually happened or whether she was just feeling the warmth of his breath on her lips.

He was tempted to deepen the kiss; that taste of Cassie was like a tantalizing appetizer to a starving man. But he wanted so much more, something beyond physical union. Raising his head, he smiled down at her. "You don't have to work this weekend, do you?"

Cassie shook her head slowly. "Why?"

"Go away with me. Give us a chance to have time together away from other people, from work, even from telephones."

Passion hadn't completely fogged her brain. She blinked and withdrew from him, leaning back and giving him a baleful look. "What's wrong?" she snapped. "Your little black book came up empty for the weekend?"

Bret felt as if she'd hit him. But at least the matter of that well-publicized date of his was finally on the table. "I only want you, Cassie," he said quietly.

"Why? Because if you don't have me, I'll be the one who got away?"

"No, that isn't why I want you," he replied in measured syllables. "And it's not true in the first place. You're feeling exactly what I'm feeling. To put it more crudely, I could have had you that very first night we met . . . and you know it."

The fact that he was stating the bald truth upset Cassie more. "Is that so?" she replied. "Well, Mr. Parker, maybe visiting Broadway stars fall into bed on command, but if you think—"

Bret's fingers curled around her shoulders. "Visiting Broadway stars haven't been commanded or even invited to fall into bed. Not with me, anyway. And now that we've finally got the subject out into the open, maybe you'll be reasonable enough and fair-minded enough to let me explain about all that."

"It's none of my business," Cassie shot back. "I have no claim on you."

A muscle in Bret's jaw tightened. "Oh, yes you have, honey. You have a claim on me just like I have on you." As abruptly as he'd grabbed her, he let her go, turned and snapped his seat belt back on, started the car, and pulled out of the parking lot.

Bret maneuvered the Porsche into a far-left lane. "There are four people in this car right now, and that's two too many," he said.

"Four people," Cassie repeated, puzzled, then blurted out, "Who's the fourth?"

Her revealing little slip of the tongue made Bret laugh aloud, breaking the tension he felt. "So you admit there are two Cassies: the lady you allow the world to see and the woman you try to keep under wraps."

These lapses were infuriating, she thought. And they'd never happened to her before. What had Bret Parker done, put truth serum in her orange juice? Too curious to fuss for long over her inadvertent honesty, she asked the question again. "So who's the fourth? Is there a secret Bret Parker too?"

"Apparently, yes." Bret paused while he made a left turn onto a main northbound artery, noting that Cassie wasn't mentioning the route he was taking. "There's the public image that I've already tried to explain to you but you seem to insist on buying anyway, and there's the person I'd like to think I am. The one my parents think I am, and . . ." He remembered Karen's pointed comments about his lifestyle. "And the one my sister thinks I could be again."

"Again?" Cassie asked, picking up on the single word, sure there was something important behind it.

"Again," he said. "Some people seem to think I've lost track of myself in the rush for success. . . ." He hesitated. Should he go on? Talk about Elizabeth? He decided to wait awhile; it was Cassie's turn for a few confessions. He'd already done more than his share. "But I do know who I am," he said firmly. "And what I want, and where I'm going."

"Not quite," Cassie muttered. "You should have taken another left at that last corner. You'll have to turn around to get back to my place."

"I know exactly where we're headed," Bret insisted. "And it isn't your place."

Unbidden excitement began stirring in the pit of Cassie's stomach. She tried to turn it into annoyance, maybe even outrage. "And just where *are* we headed, pray tell?"

"For parts unknown," he answered with deliberate vagueness. "So just relax and enjoy the ride, honey, because I've got you right where I want you now, and I plan to keep you there."

A flush began creeping over Cassie as she stared at Bret. He was supposed to be so gentle, she thought in utter stupefaction. Little Slugger's diaper-changing uncle. Maker of blueberry-muffin breakfasts. All of a sudden he looked positively primitive. Tribal. And he was carrying her off to parts unknown.

Heat coursed through her, crackling, galvanizing electricity.

Her little mental voice leaped to attention. Fantasy time again, it warned her. It was foolhardy to allow such nonsense to spill over into real life.

Cassie tore her gaze from Bret and stared out the windshield, trying to follow her voice of reason, but it kept getting lost in static, like a bad radio signal.

"You're sure you don't want to blindfold me too?" Cassie heard herself saying aloud, trying to sound sarcastic but failing miserably. Her whole body betrayed her.

"No blindfold," Bret replied, not sure how to read her reaction. He'd been ready to deal with her protests—weak ones, he'd been confident—because it was true: She did want him as much as he wanted her. She was just scared, and he meant to show her that she had no need to fear him. "No blindfold," he repeated thickly. "I wouldn't want you to miss a thing, Cassie. I want you to remember every single detail."

Lord, Cassie thought, her breath catching in her throat. He *could* read those wicked thoughts of hers. He *did* see into the secret heart of her. How could she fight a man armed with that kind of knowledge?

On the other hand, she argued silently, why fight at all? She thought of Jan's philosophy about ships and harbors and being safe. Maybe it was time to lift anchor and sail into the sunset. Off the edge of the earth, if that was the way things turned out. To use Jan's words, there were worse ways to go.

She turned to look at Bret and smiled. "So where *are* you taking me?" she asked huskily.

Bret's knuckles turned white. Never had a simple question, even in such a softly seductive voice, triggered such waves of hot, demanding need in him. He was grateful when the traffic light ahead turned red; a short time-out from driving was welcome. Hell, he thought, it was vital.

He wanted to look at Cassie but didn't dare. Not unless he planned to make the announcer in the overhead traffic helicopter come up with an explanation—one that wouldn't blister the airwaves—for the sudden delay on the road.

Keeping his gaze straight ahead, he spoke quietly. "Have you ever watched the sun rise from a cottage in the Scottish Highlands, Cassie?"

Cassie swallowed hard, her sanity threatening to return. Sailing into the sunset was one thing, but she wasn't ready to go flying off to Scotland with Bret Parker, alluring as the prospect might be. "Um . . . no, I haven't done that yet, but you surely can't be thinking of . . . I mean, I just couldn't—" She shot him a desperate look. "Good grief, Bret, maybe you and your madcap crowd can hop a jet to distant places, but I can't do it, and that's that!"

Bret grinned. He'd anticipated her panic, and she'd played right into his hands. He finally was able to turn and look at her without losing control. "Well, then," he ventured, "how about something a little closer to home?"

"How close?" she asked warily, though she was melting again at the promise in his amber eyes.

"A whole other world less than two hours north of here. Okay?"

Cassie sighed. Would she ever be able to resist his persuasive little "Okay?" Smiling back at him, she hoped she wasn't about to make the mistake of her life. "Okay," she answered at last.

Eight

Cassie stood in dumbfounded silence in the master bedroom of the picturesque country inn's luxurious suite and seriously considered calling a cab to take her back to the city. But there was no phone in the suite.

She'd spent the whole drive practically blind to the passing autumn scenery she usually loved, her whole being involved in an inner turmoil brought on by her shocking decision to launch into an affair with Bret Parker.

For her, the trip to this secluded inn had been a roller-coaster ride, her body humming with desire one minute, the next instant her mind filled with doubts. She wanted Bret terribly, never mind the consequences, yet she was just as terribly afraid he was too experienced for her and would expect too much. What if she'd kept her physical responses tamped down for too long? What if . . . ?

She'd tormented herself with countless "what-ifs," and for nothing. What had happened to the delicious ravishment she'd been dreading? Why had Bret deposited her in a beautiful bedroom and announced he would use the suite's smaller one?

How generous of him, Cassie thought, fuming. What was his game, anyway? Everything had seemed so perfect. Chopin on the car radio had created a nineteenth-century microcosm inside the Porsche amid the outside world's bustle. When an announcer's voice had intruded on the mood, Bret had flipped off the radio immediately, smiling and saying, "This is one time when no news *is* good news."

Cassie had been delighted that he'd wanted to suspend reality as much as she had.

She felt cheated, recalling their detour to a shopping mall, a lovely little side fantasy with her and Bret buying everything they would both need for the weekend. They'd even flirted playfully over which nightgown she should get. Bret's clear preference had been a sheer bit of nothing in hot pink, but Cassie had insisted on a modest blue peasant-style gown.

He'd bought overnight bags, which Cassie packed while he zipped through the mall to pick up drinks and snacks. They had all the makings of a Weekend to Remember.

Her lower lip jutted out. Separate rooms. Did the man want her or not?

Sighing, she began to unpack and put away her things in the massive mahogany dresser and the spacious closet. The inn really was lovely, she had to concede.

Nestled in a grove of trees by a lake, it was a two-story cedar structure with upper and lower decks wrapping all around it.

The suite itself was perfect: a living-dining area in addition to the bedrooms; a stone fireplace at one end of the living room, wet bar and chintz couch cozied right up to it; a mini-kitchen for fixing snacks.

Cassie especially liked one of the two bathrooms, the one between the two bedrooms. It offered a personal spa complete with sunken whirlpool bath, double-sized shower stall, sauna, and fragrant cedar tub-deck. Huge towels on a heated rack were a positively decadent touch.

The master bedroom boasted a four-poster bed with a thick log-cabin quilt, antique furniture, and a free-standing, full-length mirror.

The place was made for love, Cassie thought, wondering if she was.

She had no idea whether Bret's room was as comfortable as hers. She hadn't seen it. She hoped he had a one-inch slab of Polyfoam on a steel frame and no quilt. It would serve him right.

Water began running in the bathroom next door. Bret had said he was going to shower first so she could relax in the spa while he waited for their room-service dinner.

There were two doors in the master bedroom, one leading to the spa, the other to the rest of the suite. Cassie was taking off her dress, deciding to enjoy pampering herself, at least, when Bret knocked on the spa door. "All yours," he said with infuriating cheer.

"Thank you," she called back, sounding ever so chipper.

She chose an ordinary bath. The sensual bliss of a whirlpool didn't seem like a good idea at that moment.

The inn had provided packets of herbal bath foam, soap, and shampoo, and as Cassie sank into bubbles that fizzed around her like champagne, her mood lifted. Maybe Bret was just being a gentleman, she thought, her defensiveness fading quickly into pure pleasure.

She could hear him moving around in his room, then in the outer part of the suite. It was lovely knowing he was nearby.

Then, gradually, all sounds faded into a distant fog.

It seemed only moments after she'd closed her eyes when a sharp rap at the door made her eyelids snap open.

She had no idea where she was. Alarmed, she jumped out of bed. But it wasn't a bed, and all at once she found herself underwater, wondering how that could have happened.

Managing to clamber over the side of the tub, choking and splashing and slipping three times before getting her footing, she made her way at last to dry ground.

"Cassie!" Bret shouted, rattling the doorknob. "Cassie, what's going on?"

His voice was the clue to everything. She began to sort things out as she stood dripping all over the deck.

"Honey, are you okay in there?" Bret called, real alarm in his voice. "Cassie, answer me! Open the door!"

"I'm okay," she said, sputtering as she grabbed a warmed towel and wrapped it around herself, tucking in the end to fashion a makeshift sarong.

"You don't sound okay. You sound as if you're drowning. Will you open the damn door, please?" He began muttering about crazy females locking doors, then yelled at her again. "Cassie, so help me . . ."

"I'm coming," she said, stumbling to the door and opening it.

"You *are* all right," he said. "Thank—" He stopped talking, but his mouth remained open as a wave of relief was swamped by a tide of desire.

His heart hammered against the wall of his chest; his throat went dry. He realized, too late, that Cassie's habit of tearing around semiconscious was going to play havoc with his semihonorable intentions. So much for giving her a room of her own so she wouldn't feel pressured, he thought. So much for deciding on a hands-off policy until they'd talked their way to a better understanding. Forget that. He was going to make love to this woman, with her creamy body all pink from the bath, her shapely legs, her smoothly rounded shoulders, her maddeningly kissable lips. He was going to make love to her right away.

Her braid was still in place, he noted. It would have to go. Her blue-black hair was dripping wet and bedraggled anyway, with little tendrils plastered against her cheeks and neck. Water was dribbling into her eyes, and it dawned on him that she was groping for another towel.

Bret found one for her, wiped her eyes, and patted away the streams of water, then cleared his throat. "Turn around," he ordered, hardly recognizing the sound of his own voice as he rasped out the words.

When Cassie just stared up at him, he placed his hands on her shoulders and turned her.

His touch on her bare skin sparked a flame inside her.

Bret did what he'd wanted to do for a long time. He took the pins from Cassie's hair and slowly, carefully, with shaking fingers, unwound her braid.

Cassie had never dreamed such an innocent gesture could be so excitingly charged with unspoken meaning, so thrilling in its possessiveness.

When her hair was loosened completely, Bret took the towel again and began drying it with vigorous but careful movements, scolding as he worked. "That was dumb, Cassie. Really dumb."

"What was dumb?" she asked tremulously. Bret's fingers were strong yet so very gentle, and his closeness to her almost-naked body was turning her inner flame into a major inferno.

"Falling asleep in the tub," he muttered, enjoying what he was doing yet having trouble confining himself to the intimate, pleasurable task. "Turn around again."

She turned, tilting back her head to gaze up at him, her eyes becoming moist again—from the inside—as she decided he was the most beautiful sight in the whole world.

He continued massaging her head with the towel, watching the dark strands become a cloud of waves and curls that fell to her shoulders. His heart was bursting in his chest as Cassie changed from the loveliest woman he'd ever seen to the most exquisite creature in the universe.

"It's also dumb to lock the bathroom door," he chided without much conviction. "Especially since you obviously have a habit of falling asleep in the tub. What's the matter? Did you think I was going to attack you or something?"

Cassie looked down so he couldn't see her tiny smile. If she'd thought there was a chance of attack she'd never have been dumb enough to lock the door, she wanted to tell him.

Suddenly she realized Bret wasn't entirely immune to her. She might not be as experienced as most of the women he dated, but she recognized when a man was aroused. Bret was aroused. Placing her hands flat on his chest, she tipped back her head and smiled up at him. "I won't lock the door again," she said in a deliberately throaty voice. "Not to you, anyway."

Bret tossed the towel aside and cradled Cassie's face in his two hands. "Promise?" He wasn't referring to locked bathroom doors.

Cassie understood. "Promise," she murmured, at that moment sure she would never have doubts again about her chances of happiness with Bret Parker.

And in that instant, Bret knew beyond the slightest doubt that he loved her, that what he was about to do was make her completely his. As he lowered his head, capturing her parted lips with his, his tongue made gentle explorations, his fingers moving down the delicate column of her throat to fan out over the upper slopes of her breasts. Her skin was cool to the touch yet blazing from deep within, her mouth moist and sweet.

Cassie was dizzy with joy. Bret *did* want her! She slid her palms over the broad expanse of his chest, enjoying the texture of the knit polo shirt because he was wearing it. But his skin . . . she wanted to feel his skin. Her hands sought out the hem of the shirt so she could venture under it and feel the awesome muscle and sinew that had tempted her from the very beginning.

When she first touched his skin, Bret thought he might explode. He'd never responded to a woman so intensely, never wanted a woman so much. His kiss deepened, became more demanding, his fingers creeping under the top edge of her towel-sarong. Then he remembered. Room service. He'd ordered it thirty-five minutes before. The woman in the kitchen had promised delivery in forty minutes.

Lousy timing, he cursed silently.

Yet it didn't matter. They had all weekend. And, he hoped, much longer. Reluctantly raising his head, he removed Cassie's hands from his body and moved away from her, telling himself that the urge to hurry love didn't have to be obeyed. Waiting could only enhance the eventual pleasure.

Cassie stared at him, afraid she'd done something wrong.

Bret looked into her glazed eyes and smiled tenderly. "All of a sudden having dinner seems unimportant," he admitted. "But there'll be a knock on our door any minute, and it's probably just as well, because I have a feeling you and I are going to need nourishment to keep up our strength." Very gently, he tweaked her pert little nose. "You go get dressed. Nothing formal, you understand. That chaste nightgown you picked out and maybe the velvet robe ought to be protection enough for you, at least until we get through a meal." With a kiss on her forehead, he added, "Okay?"

Cassie nodded and grinned. She could wait, now that she knew Bret wanted her. But she couldn't wait long. "Okay," she told him just as there was a knock at their door.

"Okay," she added to herself after he'd left. "Edge of the earth, here I come."

The table was set with silver-lidded plates, pewter flatware, linen napkins, and flickering candles when Cassie emerged from her room. "I took you at your word," she said, suddenly shy again. "I wore my nightgown and robe."

He couldn't answer for a moment. He still was getting used to the unnerving knowledge that his life had been invaded by this lovely conqueror, and there she was, innocently storming the ramparts of his few remaining defenses.

Once again she seemed to be a vision, like the first time he'd ever seen her. A Galatea to his Pygmalion, created just for him by his deepest wishes. She was as magic as the night itself, her hair and eyes glinting reflections of her cobalt-blue robe, her oval face as pale and shimmering as the moon. "You're so beautiful," he murmured, hardly aware that he was speaking. He held out his arms to her.

"Oh, I hope so," she answered, going straight to him. She buried her face in the warm hollow of his throat, inhaling the familiar, heady scent of him. "I want so much to be beautiful for you."

Bret laced his fingers through her silken mass of hair and stroked her velvet-covered back. "You've always been beautiful for me, Cassie. You always will be beautiful for me."

His words shook her. He seemed to be implying so much that she at once craved to hear and feared. "What are we getting ourselves into?" she asked, her mouth brushing the underside of his jaw, her arms around his waist. "What are we doing?"

Bret wasn't sure what to say, so he stuck to practicalities. "At the moment we're about to have dinner, Cassandra, or this soothsayer will predict two disasters: cold beef and two weakened, starving people about two hours from now."

Cassie laughed when he determinedly turned her around and steered her toward her chair. She'd heard and felt the throbbing of his heart against her cheek; his self-control just added to her sizzling excitement.

"Once again you arranged a marvelous meal," Cassie remarked when they were finishing the roast beef with all the trimmings. She quickly had discovered she'd been almost as ravenous for food as for Bret. "Did you once tell me you couldn't cook?"

"I didn't cook this," he protested as he grinned across at her. "I'll accept the fact that you think there are no limits to my talent, my brilliance.

Who can blame you? But when and how would I have whipped up all that food in this suite's mini-kitchen?"

"Men," Cassie grumbled fondly. "A few stars in a girl's eyes and there's no limit to the male ego. I didn't say I thought you'd cooked the meal. I merely was reminded of your claim to culinary ignorance by the surprisingly lovely table setting. Very domestic . . . but then, that's the 'New Man,' right?" She held up two fingers on each hand and waggled them to indicate the quotes. "Tough guys playing amateur chef."

"Not this tough guy," Bret said cheerfully, pouring the last of the red wine into their glasses. "Let the latest batch of paperback detectives trade as many recipes as punches. Let them take time out from thug-bashing to perfect their pasta. I'll remain blissfully untalented in the K.P. department, thank you."

They toasted each other silently, gazes of amber fire and silvery indigo meeting over the rims of their goblets.

Cassie launched into bright chatter to cover her sudden renewal of nervousness. Just what *was* she doing there, anyway? Was it an adventure in temporary insanity or a whole new direction to her life—an unplanned direction that could lead her to the oblivion love seemed to threaten? "So I gather you don't approve of the softening of the male image, Mr. Parker."

"I neither approve nor disapprove. I'm simply admitting my own kitchen phobia. But now that you mention it, could you imagine Bacall falling for a Bogey who thought when she said, 'Just whistle,' she meant it was how he should call her to dinner?"

Poor Bret, Cassie thought, relaxing again, enjoying the silly banter. He'd walked right into that one. "I'm not sure she'd have fallen for him if he'd smelled of baby powder, either. And she'd have been wrong."

Bret's eyes narrowed dangerously. He'd almost forgotten that he'd been diapering Slugger at the time of that initial romantic encounter. "Touché," he conceded. "But I still won't cook."

"And you don't do windows," Cassie shot back. "Good thing you're rich, so you can hire the help you need."

"Why do you think I wanted to get rich?" He smiled as he thought of Cassie's remark: Bacall would have been wrong not to fall for a man who smelled of baby powder. "Tell me again how you can't stand kids," he said teasingly.

Another revealing slip, she chided herself silently. But it was one act she intended to maintain, at least for a while. She didn't dare let herself start thinking about rocking little cradles. Her longings were too strong to be allowed to surface unless she found herself faced with a very different future from the one she'd planned. "I don't hate kids," she argued, not meeting Bret's eyes. "I mean, we all had to be little rug rats once, didn't we?"

Bret nearly choked on his food. "Where do you *get* those awful expressions?" he asked, shocked but laughing. Cassie was so transparent.

"I don't know," she answered, lying. They were her father's jokingly gruff descriptions of the grandchildren he doted on. Fred Walters had a very hard time expressing honest emotion, showing his softer side. Cassie was more like him than she cared to admit. She still didn't want to mention her father to Bret.

Looking at Bret with deceptive innocence, she

persisted in hitting him with foolishness she didn't mean at all, and wondered at the same time why she was choosing to do so. "Ankle biters, rug rats," she said airily. "Would 'house monkeys' be better?"

"*You're* the house monkey, young lady. Aping someone else's act. Who's your model? W. C. Fields?"

"As in, 'Any man who hates dogs and children can't be all bad'?" Cassie shot back, grinning. But Bret knew her too well. It was scary.

The game had gone far enough, Bret decided. "Don't you know better by now than to try to con me?"

Cassie concentrated on what remained of her meal, hearing the note of seriousness in Bret's tone. "You're thirty-three," she said at last, choosing offense as the best defense. "Why aren't you a husband and father?"

"I almost was," he admitted without hesitation. "I nearly got married two years ago. Planned to settle down, raise a family . . . big or small, it didn't matter. But I did want kids, a real home, the whole bit. I wanted that very much at the time. For a while afterward I believed I'd gotten over those urges, though."

Cassie put down her fork, shocked by the depth of pain in his words. So he'd been in love at least once, she thought, wondering what woman almost had called him "husband," why the marriage had never come off, where the lady was now—and whether Bret still carried a torch for her. Was that the real reason he went out with so many different women? Was Cassie Walters just another substitute?

From the heights of joy she'd been plunged into misery, and she understood with blinding clarity how much power Bret Parker had over her. "Back to the roller coaster," she murmured.

"What roller coaster?" Bret asked gently, though he knew very well. He'd been through a wild ride himself since meeting Cassie Walters.

She forced herself to smile. "I was always happier on merry-go-rounds. No thrill rides for me. Give me a nice little painted horsie and some calliope music, and that's about as much excitement as I can handle."

"Except that merry-go-rounds don't go anywhere. You always end up back where you started," Bret responded.

"And you don't with roller coasters?"

"Not really, because you've seen new sights during the highs, and when you're in the lows you know still another zoom upward is ahead." Bret got up and rounded the table, taking Cassie's hand in his until she rose and went with him to the sofa.

He poured coffee into waiting cups before settling beside her, placing his arm around her and tucking her body close to his. Feeling her slight resistance, he realized with ever-deepening understanding how sensitive, how guarded she was. He wanted to reassure her. "The thing you have to remember, honey, is that most of the lows you've been experiencing in this particular ride have been completely created in your own head. Nowhere else. Take what I told you a minute ago about my wanting to get married: You immediately concluded that I'm still hung up on my former fiancée."

"I did not," Cassie protested, wishing he weren't quite so damned smart about her.

"Did too," Bret said, putting his index finger under her chin and tilting her head back so he could drop a quick kiss on her nose to prevent a childish "Did-not, did-too" exchange. The ploy worked: Cassie laughed. Bret was learning that he could always depend on her humor.

"So what happened?" Cassie asked, curiosity getting the best of her again. "Why aren't you driving a station wagon filled with future Blue Jays?"

"There's a certain imbalance in our relationship," Bret chided. "I share my secrets, but you keep yours to yourself. I think we need some negotiation here. I'll tell you what happened to my engagement, if you'll explain why you pretend not to want children."

Cassie winced. "That's pretty heavy stuff for what's supposed to be a romantic weekend."

"How can a weekend be romantic without honesty between the people involved?"

"Do you want a romance or an honest relationship?" Cassie blurted out.

Bret hugged her closer. "Did you hear what you just said?"

Cassie had heard. She hadn't realized she thought the two situations were opposing and separate. "I try *not* to hear what I say around you," she grumbled. "You confuse me. Anyhow, back to your engagement."

"There haven't been any promises of shared secrets from your sweet lips," Bret remarked, leaning down to steal another small taste of her.

"All right," Cassie said, deciding she was going to have to let Bret get closer emotionally if she hoped to have him be closer physically. "I'll tell you . . . some secret. Something that's equivalent to yours. Is that good enough?"

Bret smiled, ready to forego answers and just carry this woman off to bed. But her promise to share even an unnamed, vague confidence was too good to pass up. Back to Plan A: Talk first, love later. "The fiancée's name was Elizabeth Owen." He frowned. "Still is, I guess. She's the kind I once considered my type of woman, the sort I was always attracted to—until recently. The honey-haired, privileged girl who looks as great on a tennis court as at a charity ball, who's grown up believing she's a princess. From that long-ago cheerleader who laughed at my socks right down to Elizabeth and beyond, I couldn't seem to stop going for those princesses. I don't know whether it was the aura of wealth I coveted or the confidence they exuded that I envied or, as my outspoken sister Karen says, the way they looked on my arm, the perfect accessory for a successful man. I certainly didn't look beneath the surface with those ladies."

Cassie frowned, staring silently into her cup.

"You wanted the truth, right?" Bret asked, seeing her expression. "I don't blame you for being disappointed—"

"Now who's jumping to conclusions?" she interrupted. "I was just thinking that sometimes a person gets a crush at a very tender age, and when all the pining in the world doesn't make the chosen one interested, you keep finding substitutes. Maybe your cheerleader hurt you more deeply than you admit, and you keep trying to prove you can win her." With a soft laugh, Cassie snuggled a little closer to him. "That's my Lucy van Pelt number, Charlie Brown. One psychoanalysis, five cents, please."

Bret put down his coffee, took hers, and placed it on the table, then enfolded her in his arms. "Thank you," he murmured. "Thank you for making my faults look less terrible even to me." He kissed her temple, love for her flowing through all his veins. "For making me see the comic side of things. For replacing Max at Karen's engagement party. What if he hadn't gotten sick? What if I hadn't met you?"

Cassie was feeling the very same way. What if she'd gone through her whole life without encountering Bret Parker? And what if he'd allowed her to run away when her fears had prevailed? The thought made her shudder.

Bret wrapped her in tenderness, burying his face in her hair and chuckling softly. "At least we know one thing, Cassie. I've obviously broken my pattern. I didn't want to be attracted to any more privileged, tanned blonde cheerleaders. And here I am, nuts about a roving-bartender-turned-butler with alabaster skin and raven hair. It's an encouraging sign that I've dropped the old emotional baggage, don't you think? Maybe I've finally learned that princesses aren't for me."

To his surprise, Cassie's body stiffened. Twisting out of his arms, she stared at him with obvious dismay.

"What's wrong?" he asked. "I didn't mean to put you down or anything, honey. Believe me . . ."

Cassie shook her head, grabbed her coffee cup, and took a good swig. "Bret . . . I know you haven't finished telling me about your broken engagement," she said in a strained voice. "But before you go on . . . well . . ." She almost wished she could change her entire background. Bret thought she was a real Cinderella, and she was just a fake.

"What is it?" he persisted, puzzled but inclined to make light of her quicksilver mood change. Whatever was bothering Cassie could be straightened out, he told himself. "More of your jewel-theft and spying history?"

She shook her head. "If it were only that, Bret. Unfortunately, it seems to be time—past time— that I told you a little about myself." She took a deep breath, then blurted it out. "I'm afraid you've gone and found yourself another princess after all. My father is Fred Walters." She paused, watching Bret's eyes darken with shock as the truth hit him. Swallowing hard, she added tightly, "I guess you know the name."

Nine

It took Bret a few moments to grasp what Cassie had said, especially since his overriding concern was for her distress. He couldn't understand why she was so worried. "I know the name," he told her. "I'm surprised I didn't make the connection, especially when I was aware you were from up north. I never did ask exactly what town, did I? You probably distracted me so I wouldn't, knowing you."

Cassie chewed nervously on her lower lip. She'd done exactly that, she had to admit, and she felt guilty about it.

Bret shook his head. "It's amazing. Is there some kind of homing device in me that points me straight toward princesses?"

"Does it mean anything that I turned in my tiara?" Cassie asked with a nervous smile. "I've done some time on tennis courts and at charity balls, but not for ages, if that helps. I'm an honest-to-goodness, self-supporting working girl." She wished that she'd been frank with Bret from the beginning, but the fact that her father practically owned the northern town she'd grown up in and had a lot of political and business clout throughout the country hadn't seemed like such vital information. How could she have known Bret harbored a quirk about girls from wealthy homes?

The whole thing suddenly seemed ridiculous, and Bret looked so shocked, Cassie couldn't suppress a smile. "I don't have blonde hair," she ventured, then assumed an expression of eager hopefulness. "And I tend to burn, not tan," she added. "Does that make a difference?"

Bret was only half-listening. He was completely amazed at her revelation, even more so at his own blindness. Her name was Walters. She was from up north. She was smooth with people, at ease no matter what the setting . . . he should have tumbled to the fact that she'd had a lot of practice in all sorts of social situations. Even her easy grace when she got in and out of his low-slung car should have tipped him off.

But what had he seen in Cassie Walters . . . besides a beautiful woman who'd captured his heart instantly? A butler. Sure, she owned the agency, but she'd started it from scratch and had built it up gradually. There was obviously no big money behind her, so it hadn't even crossed his mind that she was anything but an ordinary career woman with an extra dash of imagination and energy.

It hit him that he'd been so caught up in seeing the prejudices of the wealthy he hadn't noticed that he had a few of his own: Privileged young ladies, for example, didn't really work. At most they were established in exclusive boutiques, if they really insisted on having careers. They didn't take real risks or go through the hardships required to make it on their own.

Cassie, daughter of Fred Walters, he mused, reeling from the obviousness of it all. There was a touch of irony to the situation that even Cassie wouldn't know about. His former fiancée's snobbishness had been based, in part, on the fact that her father was an Important Man. Why, Charles Owen had been awarded plum corporate directorships and seats on federal commissions, Elizabeth had made sure everyone knew.

Yet here was Cassie, a closed-mouthed little butler, neglecting to mention that her father was Fred Walters—who happened to be one of the backroom boys of politics who helped decide which of the party faithful got the plum corporate directorships and federal commission seats.

Life had a way of playing funny tricks, Bret thought. "It makes no difference," he said aloud, expressing a new, profound truth. "None of it makes any difference at all."

Cassie was stunned. It didn't make any difference? No difference that she supported herself, that she'd turned her back on all that so-called privilege to carve out her own existence? It didn't even help that she was a completely different physical type from the uncaring females of Bret's past?

She made the only decision she saw open to her and got to her feet. There had to be a phone in the inn somewhere, and she was going to find it so she could call a cab and make a quick exit.

"Where are you off to?" Bret asked, coming out of his reverie and grabbing her hand.

"I think I should leave," she said quietly, controlling her inner quaking so it wouldn't show and embarrass them both. "I can't begin to tell you how sorry I am that I didn't make my . . . my family connections clear before. But what's done is done, and I can't change who I am, so . . ."

Bret stood up, realizing how Cassie had taken his remark. "Cassie, you've got it all wrong. There's no call for you to leave."

The gentleness in his voice was almost her un-doing. She jerked hard on her hand, freeing it. She had to escape before she made a total fool of herself. "I've got to leave," she whispered, her throat constricted. "I can't stay here with you. Not now, Bret. Please . . ."

She was halfway across the room when she was suddenly lifted off her feet and carried as if she were weightless. When she stared up at Bret in mute surprise, he bent his head and kissed her with such depth and tenderness she knew with a deep-seated certainty that she'd read his reaction all wrong.

He released her mouth and looked down at her, his eyes as dark as molten copper. "What we seem to have here," he said with an unmistakably lov-ing smile, "is a definite failure to communicate."

Shakily, she returned his smile and twined her arms around his neck. "I thought we were com-municating pretty well just now."

"We were. Why don't we forget the verbal kind and concentrate on what we seem to do best?" he suggested, taking her into the bedroom.

Cassie nuzzled Bret's neck as they approached the four-poster. Hearing his deep, quiet chuckle, she glanced up at him questioningly, then fol-lowed the line of his gaze and saw what was amus-ing him. She'd turned back the covers on the bed. It would be easy enough to pretend she'd done it just for herself, but that wouldn't have been hon-est. And honesty was proving itself to be the best policy. "So I was an optimist," she admitted with a grin. "A girl can always *hope* she's going to be seduced, can't she?"

Bret lowered her to the bed. "When the girl is as seductive as Cassie Walters, she can do more than hope." He stretched out over her, his weight sup-ported on his elbows as he sprinkled kisses over her face. "She can go so far as to turn back the covers on the bed," he added between kisses.

Cassie's happiness was matched only by her curiosity. "Why, were you planning to sleep in the other room, anyway?"

"I thought we were going to try nonverbal communication for a while," Bret chided, grazing a pulsating chord of her neck with his lips.

"That's lovely," she said on a sigh, tilting back her head to offer him easier access. "But couldn't we have a tiny bit of the verbal kind as well? I'm a very verbal sort of person. Why *were* you planning to sleep alone? And to leave me to sleep alone in this great big bed?"

He smiled down at her. "I thought I was being a gentleman," he admitted. "You took such umbrage at my suggestion that we spend a weekend together, I decided to prove I wasn't a lech looking for a good time."

Cassie traced his strong features with her index finger and lifted her head to press a light kiss on his chin. "That was sweet," she said, touched by his willingness to spirit her away to a secluded country inn to be with her, with or without lovemaking. "You're a pretty sweet fellow, in fact."

He circled the inside of her lips with his tongue, becoming addicted to her taste. "You're pretty sweet yourself, honey."

She had more questions, and thought she'd pose them before she was incapable of speech or thought. "Exactly what did you mean when you said none of that made any difference? None of what?"

"Of anything. Of who your father is, of how many exclusive clubs you've ever belonged to, of whether your hair is blonde or black or purple."

"Purple?" she put in. "You're saying you wouldn't toss me aside even if I had purple hair?"

"Cassie, if you had purple hair, every woman in the whole world would want purple hair."

Laughing, she cradled his face between her two hands and delivered a long, probing kiss of her own. "I think your verbal-communication skills are most highly developed," she said when she'd released his mouth.

"Almost as much as your nonverbal ones," he told her, his lips still close to hers. A memory came back to him, a favorite memory. "For instance, your eyes speak more eloquently than the most full-blown orators' words. Case in point: that first night in my kitchen. I loved the way you leered at me."

"I did not leer," Cassie protested, her lips quirking. "I'll have you know I'm not in the habit of leering."

"I should hope not. If you were, I'd never let you out of my sight again."

"Okay, I leered," Cassie admitted, intrigued by his teasing threat.

It was Bret's turn to be curious. "What were you thinking that night?" he asked. "What was behind the jungle-woman expression in those gorgeous eyes of yours?"

Cassie pretended to be thinking hard, then shook her head. "Gosh, I can't recall." With a heavy-lidded, suggestive sweep of her glance down over his body, she added, "Maybe you could jog my memory somehow?"

Bret barely raised himself off her, but managed to divest himself of his shirt within seconds. He kissed the tip of her nose and grinned. "Does that help?" he asked, then gasped as Cassie smoothed her palms over his shoulders and back.

She closed her eyes as a shudder of delight passed through her. "Oh, yes, Bret. That helps. That really helps."

"Cassie," he whispered, already feeling the blood coursing through his veins. To enjoy Cassie was an unequaled happiness; to be enjoyed by her, with her special, open sensuality, gave him a whole new dimension of pleasure. As her hands roved freely over every inch of skin she could get at, Bret began to realize how different his relationship with Cassie was going to be from any other he'd ever experienced. He loved the difference.

Cassie lifted her head to touch her tongue to Bret's shoulder, tasting as well as touching him. "What was I thinking that first night?" she murmured.

Lost in sensation, Bret had forgotten he'd asked. He cupped his hand under her head to give her support so she could comfortably continue her delicate lapping at his body. She was driving him wild, and he wanted to help her keep doing it.

"I was thinking," she went on, pausing to rub her cheek over the sprinkling of hair on his chest, "that you looked like a living sculpture. My hands actually tingled to . . ." Her fingers stroked his skin, feeling the hard muscle rippling beneath the warm, satiny surface. "To do this," she said at last, looking up and smiling at him. "Mr. Parker, you arouse the most primitive urges in me, you know that?"

He was having some trouble with the iron self-control he'd promised himself he would exert when he first made love to Cassie. "I seem to be experiencing a few primitive urges myself," he answered raggedly.

Cassie moved her body against his, feeling the rigid heat of him, wishing the barriers of cloth that separated their bodies would magically disappear.

A moment later the barriers began to do just that. Bret reached down and parted Cassie's robe, then with her eager help slipped it off her shoulders and tossed it aside. "This modest blue thing you insisted on is enticing," he said as he moved to stretch out beside her, taking a moment to gaze at her. He pushed down on the nightgown's elastic neckline to reveal the gentle slopes of Cassie's breasts.

She was electrified by his touch yet soothed into a sensation of drifting on a warm sea, bathed by gentle rivulets streaming over her body. "I love your hands," she said softly as her breasts rose up to meet his fingers. "I love to watch your hands, the way you use them. . . ."

Bret slid his fingers upward to her mouth, tracing its full outline while Cassie tried to capture them between her parted lips.

"Whenever I look at your hands I want them on me, everywhere at once," she said, pressing her lips to his palm, then licking it with the tip of her tongue.

Bret felt as if she'd sent shock waves through him. "Honey, I'm trying to make this perfect for you, but I'm not as much in control as I'd like to be."

"It *is* perfect, Bret," she answered, then drove him a little wilder by catching his hand in hers and tracing the outline of each of his fingers with her tongue. She had no idea why she felt so uninhibited, so free, so strangely confident with Bret, but she liked the feeling and wasn't about to question it. She simply enjoyed it. "And don't try to stay in control," she urged him. "Do whatever you like. I'm here and I'm all yours, Bret, for as long as you want." Cassie hadn't known herself how true her words were until she'd spoken them. He was everything she wanted and needed, and she wasn't going to run away from him again. It would be like running away from the very essence of her being.

At that moment Cassie knew beyond all doubt that she loved him, but she didn't say the words. There was time enough, she thought, when she was certain he wanted to hear them. For now she just offered her love as a silent gift that asked for nothing in return but the chance to express itself.

Guiding his hand down to her breast, Cassie laughed throatily. "I should warn you," she said, not really joking, "you've stripped away the thin veneer of Cassandra Walters, and you may find the inner woman to be utterly shameless."

Bret decided to strip away more than her thin veneer. A moment later her nightgown was lying in a crumpled blue heap beside her robe. "What would a woman want with shame anyway?" he murmured, his gaze lingering on every ivory curve and hollow of her slender body. Leaning down, he trailed a line of kisses along the slopes of her shoulders while his hand began learning all her lines and textures, the expanses of smooth porcelain, the two circles of pale pink velvet at the peaks of her breasts, the plump roseate tips that stiffened to attention at his slightest touch, the dark thatch of silk guarding the apex to her thighs like a mysterious little forest.

Self-control ceased to be an issue for Bret. Cassie had granted him total control over her, and he was too lost in the wonder of her utter trust to be more than vaguely aware of himself. He was a master musician, she his instrument . . . or perhaps, he thought, it was the other way around. He was the artist, she the inspiration; he kneaded and molded every part of her as if sculpting her, yet he was awed by her perfection.

Cassie wanted to touch Bret as he was touching her, but she understood that her turn would come later. For now she relaxed in the bliss he was giving her, exulting in the joy of becoming his.

"You love this, don't you?" he said at last, sounding almost surprised. He *was* almost surprised. He'd known Cassie was incredibly sensual, but even in his dreams he hadn't imagined how completely she would open herself to him. "I can practically feel the heat flowing inside you," he murmured, bending his head to catch one reddened bud between his lips while his fingers roused her to new heights.

A convulsion racked Cassie, and the whole peak of her breast was pervaded by unfamiliar and delicious sensations as Bret sucked gently. She dug her fingers into his shoulders and held on, barely managing to speak. "Yes," she admitted joyfully. "I love this. I love . . . everything you're doing to me, Bret. But I can't bear much more. There's such an ache inside me."

Releasing the hardened berry, Bret feathered kisses over both of Cassie's firm, ripe mounds, then hovered over the waiting nipple. "Feel the ache, honey. Go with it. It's beautiful. I feel it too. It's our need to be together, to be joined and fused and made one."

Unerringly he found the epicenter of her desire, at the same time taking her mouth, delving into the moist cavern behind her swollen lips, probing more and more deeply as she offered herself to him with abandoned eagerness. Her body arched against his hand, and a sheen of perspiration broke out over her flushed skin.

Cassie's eyes were glazed as she watched Bret finally strip off his few remaining clothes and lower himself over her, parting her thighs but still holding back, drawing out the moment as if making sure they both took time to experience it fully. "You're right," she told him. "The ache is beautiful. I've had it since I first saw you, and I'll never again be free of it."

"Do you mind that?" he whispered, brushing his lips over her eyelids and cheeks while his promise of fullness hovered at the entry to Cassie's feminine warmth. "Can you live with that ache?"

She wrapped her legs around him, trying in vain to urge him into her. "I can live with the ache," she said, by now panting with uncontrollable desire. "I can't live with this emptiness inside. Dear Lord, Bret, fill the emptiness before I go out of my mind!"

He'd meant to be gentle, but Cassie's strong legs contracted around him and he plunged into her, barely keeping himself from exploding in that very instant.

Cassie heaved a sigh and smiled. "That's better," she murmured happily. "Oh, dear . . . that's so lovely . . ."

She caught Bret's easy rhythm right away, as if they'd done this love dance countless times before. "Isn't it just . . . lovely?" she said, flattening her palms on his chest and reveling in the feel of his strength over and around and inside her.

Bret smiled. "Yes," he agreed, though he might have chosen stronger words, such as soul-searing, mind-numbing, heart-stopping. "It's lovely, Cassie. Nothing in the world was ever lovelier."

"I know," she said with a sigh, twining her arms around his neck.

They floated together for a small eternity, but gradually their pace quickened as the fever mounted within them.

Cassie's arms tightened around Bret's neck. Her thigh muscles contracted. Her head tipped back and her breath began coming in tiny gasps.

Bret slid his hands under her body, cupping her buttocks and raising her for ever-deeper access. "Hang on, honey," he said. "Here we go."

Cassie cried out again and again, unaware of the sounds, unaware of anything beyond Bret's total possession of her. She was liquid heat, accepting his loving invasion, drawing him in ever further, opening and opening until she finally felt she was one with him.

She looked up at him, and as she met his gaze she exchanged a silent vow with him, felt him taking her to the edge of an unknown precipice. She gave a slight nod and surrendered every vestige of her will. A second later she was over the edge, soaring, tumbling, whirling through a kaleidoscope of sensations, not afraid of any of it because she was safe in Bret's arms.

Eventually they found their way back to earth, like two entwined feathers floating on a gentle breeze.

"Lovely," Cassie murmured again, rubbing her cheek against Bret's slight beard, deciding that she absolutely adored every subtle and obvious element of his maleness.

He chuckled softly. "Lovely," he repeated, deciding the word was right after all, because the union he just had experienced with Cassie was all about love, and nothing else.

Worried about crushing her, though he was keeping his weight on his elbows, he reluctantly withdrew from her body and shifted to lie beside her.

She frowned, not happy about the separation.

Bret gathered her into the cradle of his body, showering kisses over her face and throat, then nuzzling her fragrant mass of silky curls.

"Know something?" she asked after a contented silence.

"Depends. What something?"

She nestled closer, stroking the back of his neck and smiling happily. "I do believe I've left painted horsies and merry-go-rounds behind, as long as you'll let me ride with you on your roller coaster."

His arms tightened around her. "From this day on, Cassie, my roller coaster is your roller coaster. Okay?"

A bubble of laughter rippled through her. "Okay," she said, meaning it as another vow. "Okay."

Hours later Cassie lay in the crook of Bret's arm, her head resting on his shoulder, her index finger idly toying with the springy coils of hair on his chest. "You're not going to believe this," she said with a tiny smile.

"I'll believe anything you tell me. It's what you choose *not* to tell me I worry about. Do you have any more little bombshells? You're not British royalty or anything, are you?" he asked, teasing.

"Just distantly," Cassie replied, but couldn't sustain the lie when Bret gave her a horrified look. "I'm kidding!" she said with a peal of laughter.

Bret rolled his eyes but laughed with her because he was happy. She could kid with him all she liked. "What am I not going to believe?" he asked.

"I'm hungry. After that huge meal we ate, I'm actually hungry."

"Should I order some more roast beef?"

Cassie laughed again. The joy kept bubbling out of her. She was more contented than she'd ever thought she could be. "That won't be necessary," she answered. "I'm hungry, not starved. Only a little bit hungry, in fact. What snacks did you buy?"

"You stay here," Bret ordered, extricating himself and getting out of bed. "I'll be back in a minute."

Cassie snuggled under the quilt. The room wasn't at all cold, but she'd quickly grown accustomed to Bret's special warmth, and she missed it.

He returned carrying a tray laden with fruit,

cheese, cookies, and two tiny glasses filled with a pale gold cordial.

"What's in the glasses?" Cassie asked, sliding up to a sitting position without the slightest trace of shyness about her uncovered breasts.

Bret didn't answer for a moment, but stood looking at her, memorizing the perfect beauty of the scene so he could go back to it during the days and years ahead and enjoy it all over again.

Cassie felt only pleasure under the heat of his intense gaze, every instant with Bret giving her new, delicious sensations. The burst of freedom she'd experienced during their lovemaking was still with her, and all at once she realized her small inner voice had been stilled. No longer was some part of her mind detached, second-guessing everything she thought or felt or did.

It seemed impossible to her that the simple physical act of making love—though it had been anything but a simple physical act—could give her a feeling of being at peace with herself. Yet it had happened.

She suspected that Bret's unconditional acceptance of her had as much to do with her sense of wholeness as did the humming aftermath of love. "What are those treats?" she asked happily.

"Hazelnut liqueur," he answered at last. "Short-bread, brie, and—as you can see—fruit."

"You're absolutely wonderful, you know that?"

"And you're at heart a simple sort of female," Bret said, unable to summon more finesse in response to her shining eyes and open admiration. "Give you a thorough loving, feed you, and ply you with sweet, potent drink, and you're at my feet."

Cassie privately agreed, so she shrugged and shifted to make room for him to sit beside her with the tray between them. "Now that we understand each other," she said, "I believe I'd like to sample a cookie."

Bret grinned, gathered her into the crook of his arm again, picked up a shortbread, and held it to her lips.

"You meant the feeding part literally, then?" Cassie asked, her brows arched in pleased surprise. She nibbled at the cookie and decided she'd never tasted one so delicious.

The liqueur was next. Bret tipped the glass while Cassie took a sip, then leaned over to steal a taste by dipping his tongue into the sweet liquid in her mouth.

Cassie was delighted by the intimacy of the gesture. "I didn't realize the thorough loving and the feeding were to be simultaneous," she remarked, not complaining.

Bret picked up a ripe nectarine and turned it over in his hand a few times, inspecting it. "Whatever I do with you, Cassie, is simultaneous with thorough loving. Don't you know that yet?"

Cassie gazed at him, her eyes suddenly moist. "I've never known anything so surely or clearly in my life," she told him, then paused. Was it time so soon? she wondered. She made up her mind. It was time. "I love you, Bret Parker," she told him, surprised at how easy it was to take such a momentous step. Smiling, she said it again. "I love you. And it doesn't even scare me to love you." Her smile changed to a tiny frown. "*That* scares me. What's happened to my acute sense of self-preservation? I wasn't ever going to love anyone, but here I am, ready or not, loving you."

Bret couldn't speak at first. He hadn't dared hope Cassie would admit she loved him—not for a long while, anyway. He smiled. Taking her hand in his, he kissed the backs of her fingers, then her palm. "Your sense of self-preservation is intact," he said, his voice vibrating with emotion. "Perhaps it's even working more efficiently than ever; deep inside you know we belong together. You know it's right for you to love me. And in case I haven't yet made it clear enough . . . I love you, Cassie. I think I've loved you forever. I know I'll love you for the rest of forever."

When tears slipped from the corners of her eyes, Bret decided he'd better lighten the moment or they would both be weeping. He held the nectarine to her lips and smiled. "Sink your pretty teeth into this ripe flesh, sweetheart. Let the juices dribble down your chin so I can lick them off. Maybe I'm becoming a gourmet after all. Maybe I simply needed the right ingredients to inspire me."

Laughing softly, Cassie bit into the sweet, bursting fruit while Bret kissed away her tears, then enjoyed the dessert with a special male gusto.

When the nectarine was gone and not a drop of juice remained on Cassie's chin or breasts, Bret moved the tray and filled Cassie once again with himself, their bodies sealing the love they'd spoken.

Cassie fell asleep in the perfect comfort of Bret's arms, deciding as she closed her eyes that never again would she listen to that negative, unpleasant little voice of so-called reason that had been part of her for too long. It was gone forever, finally bested.

Ten

"What happened with you and Elizabeth?" Cassie asked during their early-morning, mist-veiled walk along a wooded path near the inn. The question had been puzzling her since before dawn, when she'd awakened to find herself cuddled against Bret, his arm around her, and his deep, even breathing an echo of her own contentment.

She couldn't imagine any woman voluntarily giving up a life with Bret, and she couldn't picture him breaking an engagement without a good reason.

"Let me go back a bit further than Elizabeth," Bret replied after weighing his words for a moment. "I told you I was forever setting my sights on princesses, completely ignoring the fact that I was a commoner."

"I wish you wouldn't talk like that," Cassie put in. "It's reverse snobbishness, you know."

Bret put his arm around her shoulders and gave her a quick hug. "You're right. And I think you're going to be good for me in more ways than one, honey. Now, where was I?"

Cassie's eyes twinkled as she looked up at him.

"You were the humble but pure-at-heart gypsy longing for the love of a lady," she said.

The comment earned her an affectionate but smart smack on the bottom. "Don't go getting too big for your cute little britches," Bret warned her. "Now, do you want to hear my sad tale or do you want to keep pushing your luck?"

"Tell me your sad tale," she answered quickly, afraid he might decide not to confide in her after all. "You kept finding yourself infatuated with young ladies who foolishly considered a factory-worker's son beneath them, right?"

"It sounds as if you could relate the sorry details yourself," Bret remarked, giving her another quick hug. "And why not? Let's see how well you can do."

"Sure. This is easy. I used to see this sort of 'in-group' thing all the time: girls in their tennis whites flirting with club waiters they wouldn't dream of going out with—even when the waiters were working summers to finance another term at law school. Parents getting all tense because Carolyn or Jennifer or . . . or Cassie seemed to be interested in a totally unsuitable fellow."

Bret felt a stab of unreasonable jealousy. "And was Cassie interested in an unsuitable fellow?"

She scowled at him. "This is your story, not mine. But just for the record, yes. Not seriously, though, and the relationship didn't go anywhere. I got the hands-off message from Mummy and Daddy very clearly, and at that time what Mummy and Daddy said, Cassie did. Now—"

"Before we leave the subject," Bret put in, "who was the character you noticed enough to give Mummy and Daddy a scare? What did he do, I mean?"

Cassie tipped back her head and laughed. "He was a cowboy."

"I'm serious," Bret chided.

"I'm answering seriously. It's the truth. In fact, he was a rodeo cowboy. We were out in Calgary, or rather just outside Calgary, staying at a family friend's ranch, and there he was, a real live cowboy. I thought he was great. He *was* great—all squinty-eyed like Clint Eastwood, strong and silent, a champion at the previous year's Stampede. What girl of eighteen wouldn't have been dazzled? And he sort of liked me, too, but I gave him the quick freeze after a long heart-to-heart with my parents. Now may we get on with the Bret Parker saga?"

Bret privately thought they'd never left it. For one thing, Cassie Walters was an essential part of his saga now. For another, it was an interesting experience to view the princess syndrome from a princess's angle. "Okay," he agreed cheerfully. "Go on."

"Okay. The girls flirted with you and you responded, but if you went so far as to suggest a date, they were busy. Or if one of them did rebel enough to start seeing you, she suddenly and inexplicably cooled off to you at some point. Now, there were dozens and dozens of less-privileged and -spoiled young things sighing over you—"

"Not quite dozens and dozens," Bret muttered. "I hate to disillusion you, but not only was I oblivious to my humble gypsy background; I'd never realized what a typically gangly teenaged nerd I was."

Cassie slipped her arm around his waist and rested her cheek against his arm, wishing they could travel back through time so she could hug that boy. "I'll bet you were gangly," she conceded. "But never a nerd. Just sweet and sincere and painfully romantic. I would have loved you, I promise."

"But Mummy and Daddy might have disapproved. What would you have done then?"

"I'd like to think I'd have defied them, but I'm not so sure," Cassie admitted. "I probably would have loved you in silence and considered myself a tragic heroine."

They were quiet for a few moments, lost in their thoughts and only dimly aware of the rustling of damp leaves at their feet, the sounds of shallow waves on the lake swishing over the rocks on shore, the drilling of a woodpecker high above them.

"Somehow those elusive girls became a sort of symbol to you," Cassie went on quietly. "When you saw yourself as a successful man, a smooth, well-dressed blonde was part of the picture. You fooled everybody by becoming a force to be reckoned with, and suddenly you were acceptable, even to wealthy parents. And then you met Elizabeth." Stopping in her tracks, Cassie spoke more gravely. "I don't know what happened then."

"I kidded myself," Bret admitted, picking up the thread of the story. "I let myself believe it was Bret Parker, the man, who'd finally broken through the social barriers. I started to think I could accomplish anything, make anything happen, change anybody's stupid, snobbish prejudices. I also considered myself a canny judge of people. I wasn't." He took Cassie's hand and gave it a tug, wanting to walk again.

She matched his stride, gently squeezing his hand. "Was Elizabeth unfaithful to you or something?"

"In a way, yes, but not how you mean. Her unfaithfulness wasn't in the form of an affair with another man. Hers was pretending to be something she wasn't. I was lucky: I found out the truth in time."

Cassie stopped again, worried. "But why would you want *me*, when *I'm* like that? When you know I pretend to be something I'm not?"

Bret grinned and pulled her along again. "Just as there are princesses and princesses, honey, there are pretenders and pretenders. Elizabeth faked feelings she didn't have. You try—and try in vain, I have to add—to deny the feelings you do have. There's a big difference."

Cassie wasn't sure about that, but she relented for the moment and continued walking. "What feelings did Elizabeth fake? She must have loved you. It would be impossible not to love you."

"Keep thinking that way, Cassie," Bret said, chuckling. "Elizabeth seemed so loving, and maybe I'd have been fooled by her indefinitely—or at least until after we were married. But what I found so special about her was the way she seemed to feel about my family. Even when I'd become successful, Cassie, my down-to-earth folks weren't made particularly welcome in some of the social circles I'd penetrated. Not that they cared: Mom and Dad, Jack, Karen, Trish . . . they would rather hunker down with a case of beer and a couple of guitars in a basement rec room than make polite party talk any day. But I won't see them snubbed, and it has happened a few times."

Cassie admired him for his loyalty, but his words stirred her dreaded voice of doubt: Hadn't she experienced enough hurt escaping the incessant demands of her own family? Why would she willingly march into another situation rife with the clan loyalty she'd begun to see as a kind of prison? "Elizabeth was different?" she prompted quietly, wishing she could still that awful voice again. She'd thought it was gone forever. Forever had lasted for a night.

"Elizabeth *seemed* different," Bret said, correcting Cassie, noticing her sudden tension, mentally going back over what he'd said to cause it. He went on explaining but was alert to her reactions. "Elizabeth made sure her parents met mine, and they all appeared to get along well. She went shopping with Karen—who, I have to admit, was never won over—and picked up thoughtful little gifts for Trish and Gordon's kids."

"Gordon?" Cassie repeated, her troubled thoughts giving way to momentary puzzlement. "I didn't meet him."

"That's right. I'd forgotten: Gord had to be in California for some computer trade show and couldn't make the engagement party. We decided to go ahead with the plans because trying to set a date that suited everyone in the family was impossible."

Cassie knew the problem all too well. She'd listened to countless family discussions where someone always ended up feeling left out no matter how many different compromises were tried. She'd deplored those discussions, knowing how they inevitably turned out. "I'm amazed," she said lightly. "That willowy blonde sister of yours is a mother?"

"Of four great kids," Bret replied. "You'll love them."

"Have you forgotten my feelings toward children?" she said, her softened inner core beginning to tense up again.

Bret grinned and ruffled her hair, pretending not to notice her gradual return to the Cassie who tried so hard to be tough and failed so badly. "No, honey. I haven't forgotten your feelings toward children," he said with deliberate ambiguity.

"Back to Elizabeth," Cassie reminded him. "She's buying presents and going shopping and getting parents together . . ."

"And, fortunately," Bret continued, "she's also

going out for chic little lunches, sometimes with me, occasionally with Karen or Trish—though never with Susan, come to think of it, even when Jack and Suze were in town. I think my sister-in-law was too much even for Elizabeth's acting ability."

"Jack's wife seemed lovely to me," Cassie protested.

"She is lovely. But she's a socially concerned, earth-mother type. She's more likely to launch into a discussion of the exploitation of third-world labor than talk about the latest fashions from Paris. Nowadays, when marching to protest the bomb is out of style, Susan's still doing it, trying to make a difference, with Slugger in tow." Bret laughed and shook his head. "Suffice it to say that Elizabeth would not have enjoyed a chic lunch with Susan, even to prove how democratic she could be."

"Why did you say it was fortunate Elizabeth went for those lunches?" Cassie asked, her curiosity piqued.

"Because she happened to be at a Japanese place one day, nibbling at sushi and chatting rather volubly with her girlfriend—she'd gone a bit heavy on the saki, I think, because she was usually more discreet—and I happened to have chosen that same restaurant for my lunch. It was a spot we both liked. I'd been scheduled for a noon appointment elsewhere, but it had been canceled at the last minute, and I'd suddenly gotten a yen for teriyaki steak."

Cassie wrinkled her nose. "A *yen* for teriyaki steak? Would you really say something like that on purpose?"

Bret chuckled. "No, I wouldn't. Have I told you lately how crazy I am about you?"

Cassie couldn't, just couldn't, resist him. Her

insides melted again. She even thought she could learn to cope with a big family if she had to. "Why won't you finish your story?" she demanded huskily.

"Because you keep interrupting."

"My lips are sealed," she promised.

He bent and gave her a hard, thorough kiss. "Now they're sealed."

Cassie smiled and found herself thinking that families really weren't so bad. Since her lips had been so delightfully sealed, she pressed them together and made an impatient, beckoning motion with her hand to urge Bret to get on with the end of his tale. She was getting a little weary of Elizabeth.

"Okay," he said. "At the time I thought coincidence had put me at the table next to Elizabeth's, just beyond one of those thin screens that give such a faulty illusion of privacy. Now I know fate sent me there. Something had to shake me to my senses so I'd wait for Cassie Walters to show up in my kitchen and claim me for herself."

Cassie forgot she wasn't supposed to interrupt. She was caught up in the scene, sure a dramatic denouement was coming. "What did you hear?" she asked, her eyes wide.

"I was about to go around the screen, when I was stopped in my tracks. My fiancée was talking. 'Nothing actually *wrong* with them, or anything,' she was saying. 'At least I don't expect them to be an embarrassment at the wedding. But really, Bret is so devoted to—hung up, I'd call it, on that family of his. Never mind. I'll wean him after we're married.'" Bret gave the words the singsong inflection of Elizabeth's cultivated voice and found to his surprise he was more amused than bitter. He wasn't bitter at all, in fact, now that he thought about it. Love for Cassie seemed to expand and flow into the spot bitterness had vacated.

"That wasn't nice," Cassie said softly. "If the woman felt that way she should have been honest with you."

"That was my thought too," Bret went on. "I left the restaurant without making my presence known, but I faced Elizabeth that night with what I'd heard. We both knew it was over between us, so Elizabeth decided she might as well hit me right between the eyes with the whole truth and nothing but. She told me how she'd never given a damn for me, how the only real assets I had were in the bank, how she'd been lowering herself to marry me only because she thought I might have some potential if I'd just grow up and stop clinging sentimentally to my—"

Bret stopped talking as Cassie threw herself at him, wrapping her arms around his body and hugging him as hard as she could. "She was lying then, too, you know. Elizabeth knew she'd lost you and wasn't ever likely to find anyone as wonderful and beautiful as you again in her whole life, so she wanted to hurt you as much as possible. And because you'd trusted her enough to let her get close, she knew exactly what weapons would be most effective. But she didn't mean a word, Bret. Believe me. Not a single, solitary word."

Bret closed his eyes and drew a long, thankful breath. Cassie was obviously nothing short of ferocious when someone she loved was attacked, or even had been attacked in the past. In the distant, unimportant past, he thought. "I've had enough walking," he murmured, burying his face in the soft, fragrant cloud of her hair. "How about you, tiger?"

She realized she'd shown her claws a little, and laughed, slightly embarrassed. But no one would ever talk that way again to Bret as long as she could help it.

• • •

They emerged from their suite hours later to enjoy fresh lake trout in the inn's dining room. Rain was drumming quietly on the mossy earth outside the picture window, while a breeze whispered through shivering leaves.

The reflected russet glow of the hurricane lamp on their table highlighted Bret's strong features in a way that fascinated Cassie. "Are you part Spaniard?" she asked. "Apache, perhaps?"

"Nothing that exotic, as far as I know," he said, roused from admiring the way her softer hairdo combined with the collar of her black knit dress to create a perfect frame for her pale, lovely face. "But I can be part Spaniard for you if you wish, or Apache, or an Arab sheikh whisking you off to my tent."

"You're all of the above," Cassie admitted. "You're also far too knowing. Take your ability to read my silly fantasy life, for instance. It makes me feel almost frighteningly exposed and vulnerable."

"There's nothing wrong with feeling exposed and vulnerable," Bret said gently. "But I'm looking forward to the time when it doesn't frighten you. For the record, your fantasy life isn't silly," he stated. "It adds an extra dimension to our pleasure. Besides, I've always wanted to be a Spaniard or an Apache or an Arab sheikh." His lips quirked in an affectionate grin. "Hasn't it crossed your mind that I couldn't read your fantasies if I'd never had my own?"

"Tell me," she urged. "Do you see yourself as a bullfighter . . . ?"

"Hold on a minute, Cassandra. Isn't it your turn to bare your soul?"

Her voice turned husky. "I bare my soul every time you kiss me or touch me or even look at me, Bret Parker."

Bret sucked in his breath, then let it out slowly before replying. "And all it takes from you is that certain expression in your eyes to make me ache to kiss you and touch you . . . and make love to you again." Summoning his wavering self-control, he returned to his meal and sampled the savory mixture of wild and basmati rice before attempting to talk to Cassie again. She had a way of making his mind turn fuzzy, he mused. Eventually, though, he recalled what it was he wanted to know. "Do you have some sort of problem with your father, Cassie?"

She rolled her eyes, wishing Bret hadn't gotten around to asking her about that. "No problem at all," she said. "I don't speak to him, he doesn't speak to me—how could we have a problem?"

Bret shook his head. "Would you like to take another run at your answer, sweetheart? Somehow that one didn't have the ring of frankness to it that I was hoping to hear."

"Isn't the rice marvelous?" Cassie said. "And the green beans must have been taken from the garden after we gave the waiter our order, I swear. . . ." Her shoulders sagged as she gave in. "Dad and I had a quarrel. Our first quarrel, our last quarrel, our only quarrel. But what a quarrel it was." She tried to sound detached, even amused, almost as if she were talking about someone else's life. "It got out of hand, some unpleasant things were said on both sides, and we haven't patched it up. That's about it, basically."

Bret wasn't about to let her off the hook with such a clipped summary. "Would you rather not tell me what this quarrel was about?"

"I'd rather not talk about it at all, if you want the truth."

"You mean, if I want you to tell the truth you don't wish to discuss it, but you'll talk if—"

"No!" Cassie protested. "I meant that the truth is, I don't—"

"I was aware of what you meant," Bret interrupted. "But your phrasing was interesting, wasn't it? Anyway, I'll try an easier question: Why is this subject so difficult for you, if you're as blasé about the whole situation as you try to let on?"

Cassie picked at her food for a while before answering, then spent several moments studying the flickering shadows on the pine walls of the dining room. "I guess you know I'm not all that blasé about it, right?"

"I guess I do know that," Bret responded quietly. "Let's back up a bit. Tell me about you and your family, and leave out the last part, where you had the quarrel."

Cassie smiled. "I guess I can handle that. Let's see; where to start?"

"Are you an only child?"

"Yes and no."

Bret leaned forward, a muscle in his jaw working. "Games, Cassie?"

She shook her head vigorously. "Not at all. I have four brothers, but they're all so much older, I grew up as if I were an only child. I mean, they weren't children anymore. I guess they were, really, but I didn't know it then. The youngest of my brothers was fourteen when I was born, his voice had changed, and he was tall. I thought he was a man. What did I know? I was just a little kid!"

Bret couldn't help smiling. "That's quite an age span."

"You're telling me. I was an accident, you see. Not one of the happiest accidents in the world, either. It was a tough pregnancy for Mom, and suddenly she was elbow deep in diapers at a time when a certain measure of freedom should have been in store for her."

"I'll bet she was thrilled to have a little girl after raising all those boys."

"Not exactly," Cassie said with a crooked smile. "Don't get me wrong. My mother was attentive and loving and kind, but . . . her mind was always somewhere else. I got the feeling she was looking at my refrigerator art and listening to my childish tales but really seeing and hearing something else entirely."

Bret remained quiet. Cassie finally was opening up, and he didn't want to take the chance that a single misplaced word from him would shatter the moment.

She took a few more bites of the fish, then smiled at Bret. "I used to go fishing with my father. Not often, but enough so I know the taste of trout cooked on a campfire. I love trout. And campfires. And—" She stopped abruptly.

Bret couldn't let it go by. "And your dad?"

Cassie scowled. "I guess so, stubborn and domineering and hypocritical man that he is. Okay, I love him." Her eyes softened as she put down her fork and daintily wiped her mouth with her napkin. Turning to gaze through the rain-spotted window at the darkened lake, she sighed. "At least I never felt he was only partly with me." As if realizing what she'd said, she went on hastily. "But it wasn't Mom's fault she was that way. She'd been a model, a New York model. Her life included flying off to Europe for shoots in London and Paris, choosing her own friends, her own pleasures. Then along came Fred Walters to sweep her off her feet, and all of a sudden everything changed. Love turned her into what is poetically called a helpmate but in real terms meant she lost track of herself."

"It happened to a lot of women," Bret pointed out gently. "Especially from the era you're talking about. Around the fifties, I'd guess from what you said about your brothers' ages."

"I know," Cassie agreed. "Then came the sixties, and those women started finding themselves again. But they usually weren't saddled with a brand-new baby when they were pushing forty, and they didn't have my father for a husband. He had a certain image in his mind of how a woman should act, how she should think and feel and *be* . . . and Mom conformed rather than fight."

"And you?"

"I conformed, too, for a long time. I was my father's precious doll. A perfect lady. I never raised my voice or whined or argued. Not twice, anyway."

"What did he do to command such obedience?" Bret asked, genuinely puzzled. His own father was of the old school, too, but his old-fashioned ideas about women had been updated by a houseful of vibrant, assertive females. Bret began to wonder whether Fred Walters had been brutal. The very thought made every muscle in his body tighten. "What did he do, Cassie?"

She frowned, then shook her head and laughed. "What did he do? He . . . he looked disappointed."

Bret's muscles relaxed a little. "That was *it?*"

"You have no idea how disappointed my father can look! You see, he's so charming. Heavens, he's noted for it, like you." She paused as her own words hit her.

Bret didn't like the pause. If Cassie started thinking along those lines, her fears would start emerging again. But, he realized, he was beginning to have a deeper understanding of those fears, and he didn't blame her for them. It couldn't have been easy having to toe the line just to avoid disappointing someone she'd worshiped. No wonder she'd been wary of loving someone else and becoming once again the tense, self-effacing person she'd finally put behind her.

Suddenly his admiration for Cassie shot up several notches. She'd broken free of the hold her father had exerted over her. Bret didn't know how, but she'd done it, even at the cost of being completely estranged from the man. "You're pretty brave, you know that?" he said impulsively.

"Me? Brave? Why on earth would you say that?"

Instead of answering right away he signaled for the check. They'd finished their main course, and Cassie had already said she'd prefer to linger over fruit and cheese and coffee in the suite. "Why would I say you're brave?" he repeated just before the waiter arrived. He paused to add a tip and sign the check, then got up to hold Cassie's chair. With his hand on the small of her back to guide her out of the dining room, he grinned down at her upturned face and quizzically raised brows. "Just call it a hunch," he said with a wink.

He only hoped she was brave enough to sustain her faith in the love they were finding together. A romantic, hideaway weekend made it easy to fall in love. Living in the real world was going to be the true test.

Eleven

Cassie stood in front of her desk, glowering, and twisting her body as she tried to inspect the back of her new floral-printed challis skirt for wrinkles.

Jan walked in with a sheaf of papers for filing, laughed, and shook her head. "No, Cassie. It isn't wrinkled. You look perfect. Bret's family will love your outfit, and who knows? They might even think you're not so bad yourself."

Cassie went over to her full-length mirror to check the skirt again, finally deciding Jan was right. There were no wrinkles. "Must've been my imagination," she muttered, then turned her attention to her sweater. "You don't think this is too bright?"

"If you were worried about bright, why would you wear red?" Jan queried with a bemused smile.

"Bret likes me in red," Cassie replied honestly. "I need all the ammunition I can muster." She went back to her desk and sat down, reasonably confident that the skirt would live up to the saleswoman's promise not to crease. "I do wish I'd worn an older outfit, though. I'm never comfortable in brand-new clothes."

"You look terrific," Jan insisted. "Why would you use a word like ammunition, Cassie? Anyone can see that the man is nuts about you. His family will be, too, but even if they're not, it won't change his feelings."

Cassie wasn't so sure. As she absentmindedly watched Jan put away the files, thoughts of Elizabeth Owen returned to worry her a little.

Had Bret's family meant more to him than his fiancée?

No, Cassie corrected herself silently. Elizabeth's insincerity and her ridiculous snobbishness had been the problem.

But would Bret have wanted to marry Elizabeth had she been honest from the beginning about her real feelings?

Cassie picked up a pencil and began doodling on a memo pad, sketching a whimsical picture of her inner, negative voice. Apparently, she thought, she'd been too quick to dismiss it as conquered once and for all.

Her voice was absolutely wrong about what might come of the dinner with the Parkers that evening, Cassie told herself. She'd already met Bret's family. None of them had seemed too overwhelming. And Cassie Walters was not Elizabeth Owen.

Jan shut the file drawer and went behind Cassie's desk to turn down the thermostat for the weekend. It was after five on a Friday night; time to start closing up the office. She glanced at Cassie's drawing and did a double take. "What's with the fire-breathing toad? Surely that's not the way you see your future mother-in-law!"

Cassie looked at her rough drawing and laughed. "No, she's not like that at—" She stopped, flustered. "I mean, if you're talking about Bret's mother . . . she's really quite lovely. But nobody said she's my future mother-in-law."

"Take it from me," Jan said. "She's your future mother-in-law. I've seen Bret Parker's eyes all the times during these last several weeks when he's come here to pick you up, and, lady, that's true love. You've found your handsome prince." Looking pointedly at the memo pad, Jan added, "What I'd like to know is, who's the toad?"

Cassie couldn't help smiling at the thought of Bret's loving eyes. She tore the page off the memo pad and crumpled it. "The toad is the real me," she retorted, her aim at the wastebasket dead on. "How's life as a blonde?" she asked, handily changing the subject. "Having any fun?"

"Enough to make me almost forget we're halfway into November, it's miserable outside, we're heading into the start of the party season next week, and I'm suffering from unrequited love," Jan shot back.

Cassie gave her head a little shake as if to clear the cobwebs away. "That's a lot of compensating for a hair color to have to do," she remarked, feeling bad about her self-absorption, her quiet moodiness over something as . . . as pleasant, really, as being invited to dinner with the family of the man she loved. "You want to tell me who your secret love is?" she asked Jan quietly.

The young woman sat down and rested her elbow on the corner of Cassie's desk, her chin on her cupped hand. "Max," she said with a look of mock dismay. "The dashing Max Webster."

Cassie stared at her for several moments, absorbing the information, then wondered why she hadn't known before. Jan's eyes did have a special sparkle when Max walked into the office, and she was always so quick to give him a call to say his check was ready or to update client data. "For all his flair," Cassie said carefully, "Max is a shy person. Maybe your feelings aren't as unrequited as you think."

"Don't do it to me, Cass. Don't make me hope."

Cassie understood, but as she went over certain small clues in her mind, she wasn't sure Jan's hopes would be misplaced. "I still say Max is shy. You're an assertive lady. Why don't you ask him out? Use the old someone-gave-me-two-tickets routine, if it helps. All he can do is say no, and maybe that would hurt, but at least you'd have given it a try. He might say yes. What a shame if neither of you will make the first move "

Jan stared off into space. "You think Max likes me as a blonde?" she asked.

"I think it's time you stopped trying to anticipate what some man will like. If you're happy with blond or red or—" Cassie suppressed a grin, "or purple hair, that's what counts. It's the only thing that counts."

Jan nodded and smiled pleasantly. "You mean, the way you dress just to please yourself, right?"

Cassie looked down at the sweater she'd worn because Bret liked her in red. Raking her fingers through her hair, she laughed sheepishly. "Well, I like red too. Always did like red. The only reason I never used to wear it was because my—" She stopped short. Because her father hadn't approved of bright colors on her. Too showy, he'd always said. Women with real fashion taste wore quiet shades. Ladies didn't put themselves forward.

Was she going to spend her whole life dressing and behaving a certain way just to please some man? she asked herself.

It made her happy to please Bret! He loved her in red—and in sapphire blue and emerald green and, come to think of it, in pearl gray. So maybe pleasing Bret was fun, not something she did so he'd love her. He *did* love her!

The toad voice didn't let that go by: Sure, it mocked. She was going to dinner at the Parkers' because it was going to be *fun*.

"Anyway," she went on aloud, "I think you should make the first move with Max. You're ingenious. You can come up with a way to allow for a graceful out if it's necessary."

"You're right," Jan stated firmly, getting up. "Time to take charge of my own life. Command my own ship."

Back to those ships again, Cassie thought as she went to the closet and shrugged into her new, white winter coat. "And if all goes well," she murmured, "you'll sail right off the edge of the earth."

Ignoring Jan's quizzical look, Cassie wished her good luck and good night, and hurried off to the rendezvous with her own master mariner.

It seemed to be a good omen that the first person to greet Cassie and Bret as they entered his parents' sprawling split-level was Slugger.

The future hope of the Blue Jays, his solid little body bundled into a red fleece jogging suit, his feet sporting white sneakers, was just learning to walk. He staggered to meet the newcomers as they stepped into the foyer of the house.

Cassie's nervousness was swept aside as she realized that Slugger had learned to propel himself forward at a mighty clip but hadn't yet mastered stopping. He was headed straight for her. Dropping to a crouch, she grinned and caught him up in her arms just before he crashed into her. The two of them laughed, and then Cassie's eyes became moist as Slugger wrapped his chubby arms around her neck and hugged her.

It had been so long since she'd held a baby, she thought, squeezing her eyes shut and completely forgetting her don't-like-kids act.

"Good thing your reactions are quick," Bret said, his voice hoarse with emotion as Cassie's guard was dropped before his eyes. "Confess, honey. Do you have ten kids of your own tucked away somewhere?"

She laughed, no longer even caring that she'd been unmasked. "Just six," she answered, blinking back tears as Slugger decided her neck was a warm, soft place to nuzzle into. When Bret's eyes widened at her reply she went on to explain. "Remember, I have nieces and nephews of my own. I was a teenager when most of them were babies, and I'd hate to tell you how many Saturday nights I spent baby-sitting."

"I guess you'd had enough of taking care of children before you were even out of your teens, then," Bret remarked, beginning to understand Cassie a little better. He wondered whether she would ever feel she'd like babies of her own. Her response to Slugger suggested she would, but she couldn't be blamed if she preferred to remain unencumbered.

She frowned, realizing that it was Bret's turn to jump to the wrong conclusion. Before she could correct his mistaken impression, Slugger's dramatic greeting was followed by the excited squeals and giggles of four more children hurling themselves at their obviously adored Uncle Bret, each attempting to stake a claim on him. Within seconds two little girls were hanging on his arms, a boy of about three was wrapped around his leg, and an older one was jumping up and down trying to show off his new baseball mitt.

Cassie never did remember to be nervous of the Parker family. She was too busy answering Karen's questions about how to start a free-lance business, telling Susan what it had been like to labor in the vineyards of France, and sharing photography tips with Bret's father.

Somehow, in the midst of the lively clan, she

felt neither invisible nor self-consciously centered upon.

As she absently tied a little girl's hair ribbon, admired a crayon portrait of herself and Bret, and swapped knock-knock jokes with the older boy, she felt that strange sensation of inner peace that had come over her the first time she and Bret had made love.

Bret was fascinated by a side of Cassie he'd never seen but had always known was there. Their drive back to his apartment was quiet, as they both were lost in thought.

They were getting ready for bed when Bret finally broached the subject that was dominating his thoughts. "I never did believe you, you know," he said as he sat on the edge of the bed watching Cassie pull her sweater over her head and step out of her skirt. He smiled as he saw her scarlet lace lingerie and her dark, lace-banded stockings. Her desire to please him was one of the many precious gifts she offered so unstintingly. Peeling off the rest of his own clothes, he moved to stand behind her, his arms around her, his fingers tracing the scalloped edge of her bra. "Have I mentioned how pretty you look tonight?"

Cassie leaned back against him, watching their reflection in the huge mirror over the teak dresser. "Once or twice," she murmured. He'd told her countless times throughout the evening how much he liked her new outfit, how vivid and dramatic she looked in her red sweater. She loved his compliments, loved the admiration she saw in his eyes when he looked at her.

"You look even prettier now," he added. With his index fingers he traced the petals of the floral design on each sheer cup of her bra, watching with satisfaction the way her hardening buds poked at the heart of the flowers.

"What didn't you ever believe?" Cassie asked, unable to let the remark go by despite her mounting excitement.

"Your whole act. I don't blame you for wondering whether you want to be tied down with children, after spending so much of your youth caring for them, but your silly attempts to make me think you really didn't like kids . . . well, you revealed the true Cassie tonight, didn't you?"

"Sometimes I'm not sure who the true Cassie is," she admitted. "The only thing I'm certain of is the way you make me feel when you touch me."

"That's a start," he said, grazing his lips over the side of her throat and the slope of her shoulder while his hands cupped and gently massaged her breasts. "And I'll tell you the rest, because I know you, Cassie. I know you as if you were part of myself."

She tilted back her head and closed her eyes, the whole length of her body seared as it pressed against his naked masculinity. "What is it you know?" she asked, her breath quickening as Bret's fingers moved to the center clasp of her bra.

Easily unhooking the wisp of scarlet lace and sliding the straps down Cassie's arms, Bret gazed into the mirror at her milky, rose-tipped globes, then tossed the bra aside and began smoothing his palms over her torso from shoulders to waist. "I know how confused you are these days," he told her with an affectionate smile. "You were convinced you were the independent type. No ties for Cassie. None that couldn't be broken easily, anyway. Nothing in your life had the mark of permanency about it: not your home, not your business."

Cassie raised her head, her eyes opening wide. "What about my home, my business?"

Bret curled his fingers around her shoulders to guide her to the bed, then gently pushed her to a sitting position. Kneeling, he hooked his fingers under the lace band of one stocking and slowly drew the sheer silk down and over her slender foot.

"Your home," he repeated, starting to remove her other stocking the same way. "Furniture that can be returned to its cardboard boxes for easy storage, library books only, a dearth of souvenirs and little treasures, travel pictures and brochures dominating the whole setting." He took her hands in his and drew her to her feet. "Those are signs of a restless spirit, Cassie."

She smiled. "You're almost frighteningly observant, you know? What about my business? What have you observed about Jeeves?"

Before he replied, Bret turned her so she was facing the mirror again. "It isn't an observation as much as it's inside information. Max Webster told me a long time ago that you'd agreed to consider his offer to buy the agency. I spoke to him recently; he said he had high hopes of making a deal with you once this hectic party season ahead is over."

A thought struck Cassie. "You aren't by any chance his backer, are you?"

Bret laughed as he rolled her swollen nipples between his fingers. "Max doesn't need me as his backer. He's been socking away money for years, just waiting for the right business opportunity. He's a canny sort of character, you know. I'm impressed that he wants to invest in Jeeves."

Cassie's interest in conversation, especially conversation about business, was waning quickly as Bret's touch performed its heady magic. She reached back to stroke the hard curve of his flanks, delighting in the way he instinctively pushed his hips forward, the increasing hardness of him pressing against her.

She remembered the mirror in their country inn, recalled her awe at seeing her pale fragility entwined with Bret's tawny strength, watching the muscles of his thighs ripple with the movements of their deep union, thrilling to the primitive beauty of his hard, possessive thrusts into her.

The sharply vivid mental image and the unexpected, quick stripping away of the last bit of lace covering her made her whole body shudder with an urgent need to ease her ever-present ache for Bret.

But he knew too well that tormenting Cassie a bit only heightened their pleasure. He took her hands and flattened them over her stomach, holding them there while he crouched to touch his tongue to the dimpled hollow at the base of her spine, then feather it slowly all the way up the long column until he was standing up again, his lips and tongue playing havoc with the sensitive skin at the nape of her neck.

"Look at you," he whispered, guiding her hands over her own body, showing her its pliant, soft curves. "That's what I see, what I feel. This is the real Cassie. No career is enough for you, Cassie. So you'll consider selling. And travel alone won't give you what you're looking for. Independence and freedom are fine for some people, but not for me and not for you, honey. We're the belonging kind."

Cassie didn't try to summon a denial. The ache inside her was taking on dimensions far beyond the physical. Her every emotion, need, and most secret dream became part of the ache. It grew until she was swollen with it, consumed by it, could sense its power vibrating through her.

Bret sensed it too. He moved her hands downward once again, slowly, at last pressing them into her belly. "Close your eyes," he murmured, crushing her against himself. "Feel and accept what you are, Cassie. You need to love without holding back or doubting, to know you're loved the same way. You won't ever be satisfied with less. I've known that for a long time, and I think you know it too." He brushed gentle kisses over her cheek, exulting when Cassie turned her head to offer her mouth with a totality of surrender he'd never felt from her before.

Cassie had the sensation of strength draining from her as passion seemed to turn her insides to warm honey, yet at the same time energy was flowing into and from her. Bret's hands radiated heat into hers. His arms, wrapped around her body, were like steel bands encircling her with a rich source of power. The hard, pulsating maleness of him promised the life force itself.

Her mouth was greedy for him. The more he took, the more she found to give. The more possessive his probing exploration, the greater her softening to give him access. And when his hands released hers, his fingers inching downward to the focal point where all her heat and energy were gathering, she felt as if he were opening a floodgate she'd been unaware of.

She cried out and clutched at his forearms, tears spilling from her eyes like the swollen stream of emotion pouring through her.

Bret himself was too close to Cassie in body and spirit not to feel what she was feeling. He lifted her in his arms, took her to the bed, and within seconds had become part of her, raining kisses on her tear-stained face, his arms enfolding her as he whispered again and again how he loved her.

Cassie clung to him, weeping from joy, so much a part of Bret now, she found every movement

and burst of new excitement in him triggering
one of her own. She knew the very instant he was
reaching his summit, and she was there with
him, feeling his mounting tension, receiving his
outpouring of love into her depths, where it min-
gled with her own.

"We have our moments, don't we?" Bret said
quietly as he and Cassie lay in each other's arms
the next morning, reluctant to get up and break
the spell that had remained with them throughout the night.

"Our very special moments," Cassie agreed, lan-
guidly stretching, her lips curved in what she
thought must be a permanent smile. "Have you
ever, in another lifetime, been the lover of the lady
who posed for the Mona Lisa?" she teased.

"Only if you were the lady in question," Bret
answered, kissing her forehead.

Cassie laughed. "You always have the right answer, Mr. Parker." She sighed happily, then sat
up. "I'm afraid reality is about to intrude on us. I
have my usual postlovemaking malady."

"You're hungry," Bret said, accustomed to Cassie's habits by this time.

"Starved. Famished. About to faint if I'm not
fed."

It had become one of their little rituals: Bret
went foraging for snacks to assuage Cassie's ap-
petite. He enjoyed spoiling her, just as she enjoyed massaging his neck muscles when he was
tired. In fact they were building up an entire rep-
ertoire of mutually pleasing rituals.

The only one Bret didn't like was Cassie's instinctive closing down of communication when it
came to discussing her family—particularly her
father.

As he went to the kitchen to put together a tray of juice and warmed biscuits and his mother's raspberry jelly, he decided that the time had come to start tearing down the last of Cassie's walls.

She was trying valiantly to pretend not to be bothered by the fact that Christmas was approaching and she still hadn't spoken to her father—and she was almost succeeding.

But Bret knew better, especially now. He'd meant every word the previous night: Cassie wasn't the independent type at all. She needed to belong, and it wouldn't be enough to belong to the man she loved. She had to keep her deep connections with all the people she loved. She loved her father, whether she liked it or not.

Returning to the bedroom with the tray, Bret grinned at Cassie's unabashed eagerness as she checked to see what treats he'd found for her.

He let her drink her juice and get her fill of biscuits and jelly. "Coffee should be made by now," he told her, finishing the last of his own biscuit. "While I get it I want you to start thinking about something."

Her guard was up instantly. "Think about what?"

"I said earlier that we have our moments," Bret said quietly. "But moments, however perfect they are, don't sustain a relationship. We have to live between the moments too. And when there are unresolved problems in one person's life—"

Cassie tried to hedge. "The only reason my apartment furniture is the temporary kind," she said hastily, "is that I don't believe in being tied to possessions."

"That's not what I'm talking about, Cassandra," Bret chided.

"Well, about children. I admit I tried to tell myself I would never want them, but that was because I couldn't picture myself in a relationship where I'd feel secure enough . . . I mean . . ." She wondered what she was getting herself into. She and Bret hadn't really discussed having children. They hadn't even discussed marriage. They'd discussed moving in together, yes. Bret had asked her to; she'd been putting him off. And in the saner light of morning, even after the mystical, primitive emotions of the night before, something was still holding her back. She didn't know what it was.

She looked at Bret and realized she was lying to herself again. She knew perfectly well what it was. "I don't know how to resolve the thing with my father, Bret. If I did, it would be resolved."

"I know, honey. That's what I want you to think about while I'm getting the coffee—not the possible solution, because you obviously haven't been able to come up with one on your own. I'd like you to think about whether you and I are close enough yet for you to tell me exactly what the problem is. Maybe I can help. Maybe not, but isn't it time you trusted me enough to let me try?" He leaned down to give her a light kiss, then left the bedroom.

Cassie lay back on her pillow, in a quandary. What Bret didn't understand about the situation was that it wasn't a matter of trust. It was a question of loyalty. As angry as she still was at her father, she didn't feel she had the right to tell a single soul what had caused the battle a whole year before. Not even Bret.

And yet . . . perhaps it was the only way.

She frowned. Why did life have to be so complicated?

Twelve

Bret stood at the window in his hotel room, staring out at the San Francisco skyline, wishing his last round of meetings had ended a little earlier. The time difference meant he couldn't phone Cassie; it was one in the morning back in Toronto.

He hadn't talked to her for three days. Between her hectic pre-Christmas schedule and his intense merger negotiations, the best he'd managed had been to leave a message on her answering machine.

Undoing his tie, he decided to order a sandwich from room service and then go to bed, though sleep had become elusive recently.

Christmas was two weeks away, and Cassie was becoming visibly tense. Bret even found himself wondering whether she resented him for suggesting she might have to take the first step toward a reconciliation with her father.

She'd left something out of her account of their quarrel a year before—something pivotal. Bret was sure of it. Whatever it was, it was making her dig in her heels, refusing even to consider waving a flag of truce. Nothing she'd talked about seemed to justify her stubbornness. She almost seemed unreasonable, and Cassie just wasn't an unreasonable person.

Fred Walters didn't approve of his daughter's business, she'd told him. In fact, he didn't approve of any of the independence she'd shown since her college years, when she'd first begun asserting herself.

Bret glanced absently over the room-service menu and smiled to himself. He felt a twinge of sympathy for Cassie's dad. The man suddenly had been faced with a whole new side of his daughter. Cassie had such a fragile, even submissive way about her, it was a constant surprise to run smack into her determination, her resilient inner strength.

Finally settling on a chicken sandwich, he called down to order it along with a couple of bottles of beer. Then he got out of his clothes and into his robe, turned on the TV, and stretched out on the bed, his hands clasped behind his head as he idly watched a senseless film that was too simple-minded even for his tired brain.

What had Cassie omitted from her little story? he wondered.

The scene that had triggered the quarrel was almost comical—close to slapstick, in fact.

Fred Walters, political heavy, had been invited to an ultraexclusive fund raiser in Toronto. He'd been in the Far East on a trade junket before the event, had flown in just in time for it, had walked into the elegant hotel suite where the dinner and cocktail party were being held, accepted a drink from a silver tray, then looked into the eyes of the server—his daughter.

They'd both been shocked, according to Cassie. It was another occasion when she'd been substituting at the last minute for one of her senior employees. Since the agency had been asked only to staff that particular party, Cassie hadn't seen a

guest list. She hadn't even realized she would be
serving a group of political insiders, so it hadn't
crossed her mind that she might run into her
father.

Bret wished he could have been behind a two-
way mirror to see the widening of Cassie's blue
eyes . . . and the steam coming out of her father's
ears.

But it wasn't funny, he realized. It hadn't been
for Cassie—not when Walters had gone to her
apartment the next day to demand she get rid of
the business that had turned her into a "glorified
servant." Not when he'd told her she'd humiliated
him. Not when his outrage had made Cassie's
own long-suppressed anger bubble to the surface
and erupt out of control.

She'd admitted to Bret that she still cringed
over the things she'd said that day, the old hurts
and resentments she'd brought up, the accusations of— She'd stopped.

That was when Bret had gotten the feeling she
was holding something back. "Accusations of
what?" he'd asked when she'd looked stricken.

"Of his being a bully," she'd said after a moment's confusion. She hadn't met Bret's gaze when
she'd gone on. "Of dominating everyone. Of living
in some distant past where his word was law,
where his wife and children were his chattel. Of
not . . . not loving anyone but himself."

Bret had seen quarrels get out of hand. He didn't
come from a family of perfect angels who never
got mad at one another. Sometimes when a battle
went too far, it was tough to find a way to get
back together, to smooth things over. But people
who loved each other always managed. Cassie and
her father hadn't managed.

Something didn't make sense.

Fred Walters had learned to accept Cassie's solitary wanderings throughout Europe. He'd lived with the fact that she'd been a laborer, a governess, a bartender. Yet he'd gone into a rage because she'd founded a phenomenally successful butler agency?

Cassie's mother had somehow faded into the background, neither trying to play peacemaker nor doing more than giving her daughter an occasional phone call that left Cassie more lonely than ever.

Bret knew a lot of high-powered men whose wives had become nonentities. He knew the kinds of things too many of those men did when they were away from home.

He had his suspicions about what had been left out of the story. If he was right, there was trouble ahead for himself and Cassie, because unless she learned to accept the fact that her dashing father was a fallible human being, she would never be able to trust any man completely. And without trust—

A knock at the door meant room service had arrived.

Bret let the waiter in and tipped him too much, his thoughts several thousand miles away.

He wished he could stop brooding; it wasn't doing any good. He'd already talked himself out, trying to make Cassie see that a little forgiveness on her part might be in order. She wasn't in a forgiving frame of mind, and since she wasn't telling the full story, Bret felt he'd reached a dead end.

It was all up to her.

Cassie couldn't sleep, despite her exhaustion. She'd gone to bed still keyed up from workdays that had become arduous marathons, and with

Bret away she missed the soothing warmth of his body beside her. She'd become spoiled, she realized as she tossed and turned, trying in vain to get comfortable. She hardly could wait until he got back from San Francisco. A week had never before seemed like a particularly long time, but the past three days had dragged on forever even though she'd been so busy.

Being busy and being interested were two different things, however. It was becoming increasingly clear to Cassie that she was bored with running the agency. The sheer challenge of making it work had excited her at first, but now she was just a caretaker, and it wasn't enough.

Bret had even spotted that quality in her, she mused as she tried curling in a ball. He'd known the agency couldn't hold her interest forever.

He knew something else, she had to admit. He knew how much it was bothering her to be facing Christmas without having straightened things out with her father.

What Bret didn't understand—because she hadn't told him everything—was how much more complicated the problem was than she'd made it sound. She'd omitted one important detail from the ridiculous scene at the fund raiser where she'd shocked her father by turning up as the butler: *He'd* turned up with a sleek young woman at his side. A woman who bore a startling resemblance to Cassie's mother in her youth. A woman whose attitude toward Fred Walters was clearly possessive.

Cassie gave her pillow a good punch, turned on her other side, and curled up again, wishing she could erase the scene from her memory. It had been more than embarrassing. It had been, and still was, devastating.

The next day, when he arrived at her doorstep, her father hadn't tried to explain or apologize.

He'd launched into his attack on her business. Instead of regretting what he'd been up to, he'd been furious that Cassie had caught him in his hypocrisy. He hadn't worried about the humiliation of being seen with another woman by his daughter. He'd been upset that his cronies had seen his daughter as a servant.

Rolling onto her back, Cassie folded her arms over her eyes as if to block out the ugly memory. "You turned my mother into a—a satellite!" she'd shouted, the first time in her life she'd ever shouted at him. At anyone. "Mom's existence had to revolve around you because you're the great, the important, the powerful Fred Walters. And now that there's almost nothing left of the person you loved in the first place, you figure you have the right to trade her in on a newer model!"

Cassie felt her stomach knotting up, as it always did when the scene replayed itself in her mind. Somehow she still couldn't absorb the reality that had replaced her illusions. She couldn't believe closeness and affection could so suddenly become estrangement and bitterness.

How could Bret understand that it was impossible for her to take the first step? What was she supposed to do, say she was wrong, accept her father's right to have an affair, become an accomplice in lying to her mother?

She'd done so already. That was what had hurt her the most. The whole family had taken her father's side, shocked that quiet little Cassie had suddenly turned on Daddy because he'd asked her to give up her eccentric business and come home. And Cassie hadn't been able to defend herself without causing her mother the terrible pain of knowing of her husband's infidelity.

She had to admit she'd turned on the man, though. From somewhere deep inside had come one resentment after another, years of suppressed anger bursting out, stunning them both with its intensity.

He'd stared at her in shock. "I didn't realize you felt that way about me," he'd said at last. Then he'd left, and Cassie hadn't seen or spoken to him since.

She couldn't understand why her shattered relationship with her father mattered so much to Bret. It wasn't as if she compared one man with the other. Maybe she'd done that at first, but not anymore. She trusted Bret.

And, she recalled, forcing her mind to happier thoughts, she'd found a whole new family in the Parkers. They were fun and affectionate, and she felt so much at home with them, she was going to have dinner at their place the next night, while Bret was still in San Francisco.

Maybe eventually she and her own family would get back together, but in the meantime there was no reason to think her problems with them had the slightest effect on her life with Bret.

Mrs. Parker looked distinctly uncomfortable. One glance at the striking blonde sitting in the living room with an attitude that suggested she'd been in the house many times before, and Cassie knew. She didn't even need an introduction. The woman was Elizabeth Owen.

Cassie felt her measure being taken. She tried not to let herself wilt. If Bret had wanted Elizabeth, she told herself, he'd have had her.

But Elizabeth seemed to be on such friendly terms with Bret's folks. What was she up to? Could she win him back if she really tried? Dear heaven, she was so smooth, so attractive, so confident!

Somehow Cassie contained her panic for the whole evening. When she went home she wanted to scream at her answering machine even though it gave her another loving message from Bret. A message wasn't enough! Were his meetings really taking up so much time, he couldn't phone her during the day, when he knew she was at the office? Or was there something else? Someone . . . She stopped before she even finished the thought, realizing with a sickening thud that Cassie Walters was being as negative as ever. All the love Bret had showered on her during the past months hadn't changed her a bit. She still was expecting betrayal.

Bret deserved better.

Cassie was in her office by five the next morning, working feverishly on the day's administrative essentials. At eight she phoned a temporary secretarial service to hire help for Jan, called a part-time butler, and rearranged the schedules to free Max to work in the office, then got in touch with both Max and Jan to explain that she was leaving them in charge—she wasn't sure for how long.

By eleven she was on her way to the airport, the departures level.

Bret called Cassie at three that afternoon. He'd managed to wrap things up early and was heading home, and could hardly wait to tell her. But Cassie wasn't at the office, Jan explained. She'd left town suddenly. No one knew where she'd gone. She hadn't said when she'd be back.

As soon as he was back in his apartment, Bret tried Cassie's place, and got her usual message.

He tried his mother, remembering that Cassie had been invited for dinner with his folks the previous night.

A few minutes later he hung up, all at once drained of energy. He couldn't believe Cassie would walk out on him just because Elizabeth had decided to make a new play for him through his family.

Trust, he thought. It all came down to a question of trust, and Cassie couldn't get past her fears to trust him or their love.

He wanted to find out where she'd gone and drag her back, if necessary. Somehow he'd get it through her head that he wasn't her father or any other man, that he belonged to her and she belonged to him.

It was no use, he realized immediately. He couldn't force her to trust him. If she could leave him with so little provocation after what they'd shared, perhaps it was time to let her go.

Two days later he was trying to read the Sunday papers, seeing nothing but a blur of words on the page. Somehow he'd kept hoping he would hear from Cassie, but she'd dropped out of sight.

She was probably working as a farmhand somewhere in the Outer Hebrides, he thought fondly, still unable to feel anything but unquenchable love for her.

He was in the kitchen pouring himself a second cup of coffee when he heard a knock at his door.

The paper boy, he thought, and dug in his jeans pocket for change, then opened the door.

Bret's heart hammered against his chest as he lost himself in Cassie's sweet smile.

"Hi," she said quietly, her gaze slowly taking in his two-day-old beard and rumpled hair. Apart from those endearing details, he was dressed exactly as he'd been the first time she'd seen him: in faded jeans and nothing else. He looked even better to her now. "There was a message from you on my machine. You got back from San Francisco early."

"Two days early," he said, his voice hoarse with emotion. "I pushed the negotiations through so I could get back to my girl. But for some reason she'd disappeared."

"She had some important things to do. But she's back now." Cassie held up the plastic shopping bag she was carrying. "With the ingredients for mimosas, if you're interested."

"I thought you preferred straight orange juice," he said, his head swimming as he tried to take in the fact that Cassie really was standing before him, her indigo eyes as luminous with love and desire as ever—perhaps more than ever.

"As a rule, yes," she answered. "But I was hoping for a celebration."

It finally dawned on Bret that she still was standing in the hallway. He stepped back, wanting to pull her into his arms but holding back, waiting to be sure. "What's the celebration?"

"First, that you're home," she answered, then put down the plastic bag and her purse, quickly removed her coat, tossed it onto a hook on the coatrack, and returned to stand close to Bret. She held up her two hands, palms together. "It's cold out," she said softly. "And I forgot to wear my gloves."

He enclosed her hands in his palms, searching her eyes, daring to hope.

Cassie gazed into the amber depths that bathed her in warmth. "I missed you. And if I'd known your plans to come back early, I'd have called to let you know where I was. My little . . . pilgrimage seemed too private to explain to anyone else, even Jan. I'm sorry if I worried you. It never occurred to me you'd get home ahead of me."

He cleared his throat. "I thought . . . after you'd seen Elizabeth at the house . . ." He shook his head. "*Now* who's been jumping to conclusions?" he admitted.

"My hands are warm enough now," Cassie said, freeing them so she could indulge the desire that had hit her the instant Bret had opened the door. Smoothing her palms over his shoulders, his rigid breastbone, his flat nipples, she closed her eyes and exulted in the fact that she could walk up to him and take such lovely liberties. "I don't blame you," she told him, sliding her hands around his waist and resting her cheek against the hair-roughened center of his chest. "I'd have jumped to the same conclusions. And in a way you weren't that far wrong. I did panic when I saw Elizabeth, but only for a while. Just long enough to make me realize what you've been trying to tell me all along: I couldn't hang on to my anger against my father and still be free to love you the way you deserve to be loved. I had to let go of the anger. I had to try to restore that relationship." She looked up and smiled triumphantly. "So I did."

Bret's arms instinctively had crept around her, but he grabbed her shoulders and set her away from him, staring at her in hopeful surprise. "You did? You saw your father? Talked to him?"

Cassie nodded. "That's the other reason for a celebration. I also brought fresh croissants and cheese. Even though I haven't been made love to for a whole week, I'm hungry. I flew in this morning and didn't eat breakfast on the plane. So, if we can go to the kitchen . . ."

Bret grinned and hugged her very hard, then grabbed the bag she'd brought and put his arm around her shoulders, his lips pressed to her temple as they walked. "There's not another woman in the world like you," he whispered, his throat still constricted with emotion.

Cassie turned her head and caught his lips with hers. Suddenly she laughed. "You're scratchy."

"I'll go shave," he said immediately. "I've had a lot of showers—cold ones—but I haven't bothered with my grooming, I guess."

"I like you scratchy," Cassie told him, rubbing her cheek against his as they went into the kitchen. "Don't go shave. Don't go anywhere. Stay close to me."

"Always," he promised.

They took their mimosas and breakfast out to the solarium. Though it was a cold winter day, the sun was streaming through the wall of windows, filling the small room with warmth.

"That dress is one of my favorites," Bret said as they sat down, his gaze greedily taking in the way the sapphire-blue angora creation shimmered over her slender form.

"I know," Cassie said, her eyes dancing. "I find I enjoy pleasing you. And for some reason I don't feel as if I'm becoming a nonperson by doing so."

"We're making progress," he said, finally beginning to relax in the knowledge that Cassie was back. She'd never been away, really, any more than he had. But she'd given him a scare. "And speaking of progress . . . you really did resolve things with your dad?"

"Let's say we've made a start. A new start." She paused to reach across the table and take Bret's hand. "I didn't tell you everything," she admitted.

"I know," he said. "But you had a pretty good reason, right?"

"You even knew that?" Cassie asked, laughing.

"I don't think I'll ever try to hide anything from you. I couldn't."

"Nor I from you," Bret said gravely.

Cassie took his statement as a promise, and believed him. Then she explained the part of the story she'd omitted. "Dad insists it wasn't an affair," she told Bret after she'd filled in all the missing details. "He admitted he'd been flirting with the idea—and with the young lady in question—but running into me had made him see the whole thing for exactly what it was. Cheating. Unfortunately that clarity of vision wasn't his first reaction." Cassie shook her head, remembering the battle, still wishing some things hadn't been said, but finally sure she and her father could put it all behind them.

"How did you approach him?" Bret asked. "Two days ago, I mean. What did you do?"

"I went to his office and asked him to have lunch with me. He surprised me by accepting. You were right, Bret. Someone had to make the first move, and in the long run it really didn't matter who it was." She brought his warm, strong fingers to her lips. "As you said, forgiveness goes a long way. I told Dad I'd quit thinking he had to be some perfect, superhuman hero, if he'd quit trying to pretend to be just that."

Bret chuckled. "A tall order on both sides." He thought of something else. "How are things with your mother, then?"

"She still doesn't know about Dad's little flirtation, and there's no reason for her to find out. You know something? Dad told me I'd hit him with some truths about the way his demands on Mom had eroded her personality. He says he's trying to be more thoughtful of her. Now, I don't exactly think he's going to turn into Mr. Sensitive, but if he tries even a little bit, maybe something good has come out of all this."

"I'm so proud of you," Bret told her. "'What you did took courage and . . . generosity."

"It wasn't entirely unselfish," she admitted freely. "When I went into that awful spiral because Elizabeth turned up, I realized it was time I grew up. Or, as Jan would say, time I took command of my own ship. It worked for her, you know. She and Max are an item. Which is good, because they'll make a fine team, running the Jeeves agency."

Bret picked up his glass and took several thoughtful sips, not sure what Cassie was going to hit him with next. "And why will they be running it?" he asked.

"Because I'm going to sell controlling interest to Max. I'll hold enough shares to enjoy the fruits of my early labors, but I'm ready to move on to a new adventure."

"Any idea precisely what adventure?" Bret asked carefully.

"Another business," Cassie said, biting into a croissant as she remembered she was starving. "There are so many multinational companies nowadays, I see a need for people to learn the customs and habits of various countries. I guess you'd call it international etiquette, really. I'll hire experts on the different cultures and offer seminars, individual lessons—I still have to work out all the details, but I think it's a germ of an idea whose time has come." She laughed quietly. "You know, I've been ready to sell to Max for ages, but part of the reason I haven't done it is pure stubbornness. My father's demands that I get rid of the business made me keep it longer than I wanted to. There are ways and ways of being dominated by someone, it seems. I'm glad, though, because I met you."

"You're sure you want to sell, honey? To start over?"

Cassie nodded. "I don't like the day-to-day operational details of business. I'd rather be a catalyst. I enjoy making things happen—the same as you do, but on a smaller scale."

"The smaller scale is only for now," Bret said with a laugh, enjoying Cassie's enthusiasm. "I have a feeling Mrs. Parker will soon replace Mr. Parker in the business magazines as entrepreneur *extraordinaire*."

"I'll try my best," Cassie said happily. It was several seconds before she realized exactly what he'd said. "Assuming," she added hesitantly, "the Mrs. Parker you were referring to is me. Will be me, I mean."

Bret stood and walked around the table to take her hands and pull her to her feet. "Will be you," he stated firmly. "Assuming you'll have time for marriage while you're building your corporate empire."

Cassie smiled. "I'm pretty efficient. A human time-and-motion study, remember?" She grew more serious. "But if I can't manage everything, Bret, the corporate empire will have to go. I'm not my mother or anyone else. I know what counts for me, and, by keeping my priorities in order, there's no danger I'll become a nonperson. And you're right up there at the top of the list." Her eyes grew moist. "I love you so much, Bret."

He released her hands and slid his arms around her. "And I love *you* so much, Cassie. You're right up there at the top of my list of priorities too. Corporate empires are great, but they don't matter a whit in comparison to what we have together." He held her close, exulting in the moment he'd almost thought would never happen, then touched his lips to Cassie's ear and went for the final brass ring. "Maybe we can even find time to make a little ankle-biter or two along the way," he murmured.

Cassie tipped back her head and gave him a fierce look that was belied by the sparkle in her dancing blue eyes. "Bret Parker," she said, scolding him, "where *do* you get such dreadful expressions for the adorable little babies you and I are going to have?"

THE EDITOR'S CORNER

I am delighted to let you know that from now on one new LOVESWEPT each month will be simultaneously published in hardcover under the Doubleday imprint. The first LOVESWEPT in hardcover is **LONG TIME COMING,** by Sandra Brown, which you read—and we hope, loved—this month. Who better to start this new venture than the author of the very first LOVESWEPT, **HEAVEN'S PRICE**? We know that most of you like to keep your numbered paperback LOVESWEPTs in complete sets, but we thought many might also want to collect these beautifully bound hardcover editions. And, at only $12.95, a real bargain, they make fabulous gifts, not only at this holiday season but also for birthdays, Mother's Day, and other special occasions. Perhaps through these classy hardcover editions you will introduce some of your friends to the pleasures of reading LOVESWEPTs. When you ask your bookseller for the hardcover, please remember that the imprint is Doubleday.

Next month's simultaneously published hardcover and paperback is a very special treat from Fayrene Preston, the beginning of the trilogy *The Pearls of Sharah*. In these three LOVESWEPTs, a string of ancient, priceless pearls moves from person to person, exerting a profound effect on the life of each. The trilogy opens with **ALEXANDRA'S STORY**, LOVESWEPT #306 (no number, of course, on the hardcover edition). When Alexandra Sheldon turned to meet Damon Barand, she felt as if she'd waited her whole life for him. Damon—enigmatic, mysterious, an arms dealer operating just barely on the right side of the law—was the dark side of the moon beckoning Alex into the black satin night of his soul. But was it the woman he was drawn to? Or the impossibly beautiful and extravagantly valuable pearls she wore draped on her sensual body? This fascinating question answered, you'll be eager, we believe, for the two *Pearls of Sharah* romances to follow: in April, **RAINE'S STORY**; in June,

(continued)

LEAH'S STORY. You can count on the fact that all three books are breathlessly exciting reads!

Get ready for an offering from Judy Gill that's as poignant as it is playful, LOVESWEPT #307, **LIGHT ANOTHER CANDLE.** Sandy is rebuilding her life, at last doing the landscaping work she loves, when Richard Gearing comes bumping into her life. For Rick it is love at first sight; for Sandy it is torment from first encounter. Both had suffered terribly in their first marriages, and both are afraid of commitment. It takes her twin daughters, his young son, and a near tragedy to get these two gorgeous people together in one of the best surprise endings you'll ever hope to see in a love story.

Here comes one of the most original and thrilling romances we've published—**NEVER LET GO,** LOVESWEPT #308, by Deborah Smith. We're going to return to that super couple in **HOLD ON TIGHT,** Dinah and Rucker McClure. Their blissful life together has gone sadly awry— Dinah has disappeared and Rucker has been searching for her ceaselessly for almost a year. He finds her as the book opens, and it is a hellish reunion. Trust shattered, but still deeply in love with Dinah, Rucker is pulled into a dangerous, heart-wrenching chase for the woman he loves. Filled with passion and humor and surprises, this story of love regained is as unique as it is wonderful.

Please give a *big* welcome to a brand-new author, Lynne Marie Bryant, making her publishing debut with the utterly charming **CALYPSO'S COWBOY,** LOVESWEPT #309. When Smokejumper Caly Robbins parachuted onto the wilderness ranch, she expected to fight a fire—not to be swept into the arms of one thoroughly masculine, absolutely gorgeous black-haired cowboy. Jeff Adams was a goner the minute he set eyes on the red-haired, petite, and feisty lady. But her independence and his need to cherish and protect put them almost completely at odds . . . except when he was teaching her the sweet mysteries of love. A rich, vibrant love story from an author who writes authentically about ranchers 'cause she is one!

(continued)

Helen Mittermeyer follows up her thrilling **ABLAZE** with another hot romance next month, **BLUE FLAME, LOVESWEPT #310**, in which we get Dev Abrams's love story. Dev thinks he's hallucinating when he meets the shocked eyes of the only woman he has ever loved, the wife who supposedly died a few years before. Felicity, too, is stunned, for Dev had been reported killed in the middle of a revolution. But still burning brightly is the blue flame of their almost savage desire for each other, of their deep love. In a passionate and action-filled story, Dev and Felicity fight fiercely to reclaim their love. A must read!

Patt Bucheister gives us one of her best ever in **NEAR THE EDGE, LOVESWEPT #311**, the suspenseful tale of two people who were meant for each other. Alex Tanner had agreed to guard the daughter of a powerful man when fate made her the pawn in her brother's risky gambit. But the passion whipping between him and Joanna Kerr made it almost impossible for him to do his job. Set in Patt's native land, England, this is a very special novel, close to the author's heart . . . and, we suspect, one that will grow close to your heart, too.

Altogether a spectacular month ahead of great LOVESWEPT reading.

Warm good wishes,

Carolyn Nichols

Carolyn Nichols
  Editor
LOVESWEPT
Bantam Books
666 Fifth Avenue
New York, NY 10103

THE DELANEY DYNASTY

Men and women whose loves and passions are so glorious it takes many great romance novels by three bestselling authors to tell their tempestuous stories.

THE SHAMROCK TRINITY

THE DELANEYS OF KILLAROO

Now Available!
THE DELANEYS: *The Untamed Years*

Special Offer
Buy a Bantam Book
for only 50¢.

Now you can have Bantam's catalog filled with hundreds of titles plus take advantage of our unique and exciting bonus book offer. A special offer which gives you the opportunity to purchase a Bantam book for only 50¢. Here's how!

By ordering any five books at the regular price per order, you can also choose any other single book listed (up to a $5.95 value) for just 50¢. Some restrictions do apply, but for further details why not send for Bantam's catalog of titles today!

Just send us your name and address and we will send you a catalog!